Cherisse M. Havlicek

# Carolyn's Christmas Carol

## A Present / Past Saga

By

Cherisse M Havlicek

Cherisse M. Havlicek

# DEDICATION

I dedicate this novel to those who have loved me unconditionally. First were my parents Doris and Andy Basile. Then came my husband, Allan. He showed me a real love that surpasses any work of fiction.

\*\*\*\*\*\*

# ACKNOWLEDGEMENTS

I would like to thank my family.  Allan, my husband, Arthur, my son and Alisse, my daughter.  I need to thank my husband's caregiver Lori W.  Without her help, I would have had no time to breathe, let alone write.  I need to thank my friends, Carol H., Beth A. and Carol B. who helped me trouble shoot with lots of ideas.  I would also like to thank Marrie H. and Anne V. who read and criticized many chapters and helped me get away from it all from time to time.  I cannot forget to thank my many beta-readers.  Ladies, you inspire me to keep going!

*****

This novel is a work of my imagination.  The towns of EL Dorado and Lawrence in Kansas are real.  I have used them as a backdrop in each novel in my A PRESENT / PAST SAGA series.  Every person, name, character, event and incident in them are made up to entertain.  Any resemblance to actual persons, living or dead, is purely coincidental.

Cherisse M. Havlicek

# ONE

## Friday, December 1ˢᵗ, 1882 in EL Dorado, Kansas

Grant doesn't want to do it. *This will break her heart.* The wind is biting his face as he rides into town with all the speed that his horse Romeo can go. He reaches Central Avenue just before his face freezes off, he thinks. Snow is falling and the sun is blocked by clouds giving his mission a gloomy feeling. He jumps down off Romeo and quickly ties him up. With steps of purpose, he walks into the Western Union office. "I need to send a telegram," He says breathlessly. "It's a matter of life and death." *God forgive me for what I am about to do,* he thinks.

With the deed done, the nearly six-foot-tall, dark haired Grant gets back on Romeo. "Home, boy, no need to rush now. I am in no hurry." Romeo shakes his head, and Grant gives him 'click-click' sound to go with a kick to the ribs to make the horse move.

Once home on his plantation, he brings his horse directly into the stable, and takes the saddle off, and brushes him down. He gets a feed bag for him. He gives a nod to Clarence, his Negro stable man. Thought cold and wet from the snowfall, he goes over to his pride and joy – his racehorse, Joan of Arc, to check on her progress. A year ago in September, he took her to Lawrence for the Bismarck Grove Exposition of the Western National Fair Association's Derby. She took first place and his fiancée, Carolyn, was thrilled to be by his side for the award ceremony. The horse is young and was strong until now. Joan of Arc is getting close to the time of her first foaling, which has put her in some discomfort from the size of the foal. The newborn will be a present to his bride. *If I still have a bride, after that telegram,* he thinks. Grant then turns up the collar of his overcoat, and hurries back into the snowy cold to go up to the Farmhouse.

The house is empty except for Clarence's wife Annabelle and their seven-year-old daughter Matilda. Annabelle was born a slave, but when Grant's father Steven bought her in 1860 in

**7**

Missouri, he set her free. Then he hired her as a house servant. Steven made several buying trips to the slave market and freed - then hired the negroes that he purchased including Clarence. Grant's mother Mary said that her husband did it, in part, to make HIS father mad. Theodore Johnson thought that spending good money on worthless people, then never getting his money back through their labor or selling, was a flagrant slap in the face of aristocracy. Steven did not care. His father had remarried just three weeks after his mother's death, and immediately had three children with the other woman. Steven felt that was a flagrant slap to his dead mother. Grant would have loved to get to know his brave father, but he died for the Union at Gettysburg when Grant was only eight years-old.

After her husband's death, Mary was trapped living with her father-in-law who did not like her and his equally unpleasant wife. When Mary's mother Marilyn married Clyde Lewis in Lawrence, it seemed like a wonderful idea to take her son and daughter to live near grandparents who were loving and kind. When the twice-widowed Theodore died in 1876, Grant was the one to inherit the Plantation (being the first-born male of the first-born male), much to the dismay of his half-uncles who were married and living on their own.

Grant grumbles past Annabelle. The large black woman meets him at the back door. "I iz gonna put supper on. Does ya need anythin' from ole Annie b'fore I'z gets started?" She knew he was scheduled to be in Lawrence tonight, and should have left EL Dorado days ago. She wants to ask why he didn't go, but . . . it isn't her place to question him. She can tell he is in a foul mood, and he doesn't want a conversation even before he shakes his head with a grunt, and turns away from her to walk into his study.

Annabelle just stares at her young employer. He is taller than her 5'9" husband. Master Grant is never like this. He is always respectful when dealing with his servants. He was in great spirits about his upcoming nuptials. He saw his mother off to Lawrence, happily, knowing that she was going to help his Grandmother Marilyn make the dress that his bride will wear on their wedding day. How things went from that to this is a mystery to Annabelle. She shakes her head, and turns to go into her kitchen with a 'tsk-tsk' sound escaping her lips.

# TWO

## Friday, December 1st, 1882 in Lawrence, Kansas

Carolyn is wearing her wedding dress for another round of alterations. When Grandmother Marilyn isn't pinning her, she is swirling around to watch the full skirt swoosh and sway in the mirror. "Isn't it the most beautiful dress, Grandmother?"

"I must admit, I am rather fond of the job that I am doing. Now hold still. I swear all this energy is just wasted on the young!"

"I cannot hold still! I am to be married in three weeks! The Eve of Christmas Eve! What a wonderful day to be wed, don't you think?" She swirls around once more.

"Carolyn, if you don't hold still, this won't be ready! I still need to work on your ball gown. I think you might want that finished to wear for tomorrow's ball. Don't you?"

Mary Caldwell Johnson comes into the room. "My darling, you are going to make the most beautiful bride for my son." She has her hands up to her face, as tears start to come to her eyes.

"Please don't cry, Mother Mary. Don't ruin this by tears. Grant hates women who cry! He told me that several times. We must do everything to make Grant happy, if we can."

"Speaking of Grant, what time is he getting here? Or will he go straight to the Colonel's?" Her soon-to-be mother-in-law asks.

"He'd better not! He promised me he would come to my house for a visit before going to my brother Will's."

Carolyn's older sister Marjorie comes rushing into the small house of Clyde and Marilyn's. "Carolyn, there is a telegram for you! I brought the man here with it. It is from Grant." She rushes out all the words, and is flushed with color.

Carolyn leaves the small bedroom, and approaches the telegram messenger. She stands to her full height of 5'8", and says very formally, "I am Carolyn Lewis. You have a telegram for me?"

"Yes ma-am! Sign here." As she does so, she can feel the stare of the young man. He is a year or two older than her

17 years and quite good looking, but Carolyn is too upset to think anything other than *'Why do I have a telegram from Grant?'*

She turns away from the young man, and rips open the envelope. Her sister, her grandmother, and her soon-to-be mother-in-law are all watching her mouth the words that she is reading. Carolyn takes a step or two to plop into a tufted chair. A pin or two must have caught her. "Ouch, that hurts!" She wiggles. "Grandmother, please, get me out of this damn dress!" She stands back up, and hurries to the bedroom with the two older women following close behind her, and they close the door.

Marjorie is left with the messenger. "Sorry, let me give you something." She says awkwardly as she goes into her pocket, and brings out a small coin purse. She digs out a couple of coins. She nervously smiles at the young man. "This is all that I have. Sorry. Richard? Isn't it?"

"You remember me, Marjorie? I mean Miss Lewis?"

"Yes, of course, I do. You were a year ahead of me in school, but I remember you. You can call me Margie, Richard."

"So, your sister is getting married?" He nods toward the closed bedroom door.

"She is, I think. I guess it depends on what that telegram said. He was supposed to be here today to take her to the ball tomorrow night." Marjorie explains, but she is dying to go into the bedroom and learn the news.

"Will you be there?"

"Um, what, Richard?" Her attention is on the closed bedroom door.

"I asked if you'd be at the Ball? I wasn't going to go, but if you'll be there, I could change my mind."

This makes Marjorie turn and look at him. He is several inches taller than Carolyn, so he must be at least six-foot tall, very handsome with dark hair and eyes that are twinkling at her. A small smile shows at the corners of her mouth and a large red blush goes up her neck. *"Oh, my."* She says, under her breath, then out loud she says, "Since my brother, Colonel William Clyde Lewis, is hosting the ball, again, my whole family will be there."

"Good, I will see you there. I hope that you will save me

a spot on your dance card, then." He nods to her, and walks to the door. With his hand on the knob, he says, "Until then, Miss Lewis." He gives another nod, and walks backwards out of the cabin, and closes the door very slowly.

Marjorie stares wistfully at the closed entrance door for just a second, when the bedroom door swings open behind her, and Carolyn rushes through. "Carolyn, what is going on? What does the telegram say?" She manages to ask her sister, who rushes past her.

"Oh, not much! It just says that he is going to be delayed two or three weeks. With no explanation, at all. We are getting married in three weeks! He is not even forthcoming if he is going to be here for his own wedding!"

Mary, dark haired and petite, comes rushing out of the room. "Did the telegram man leave? I would have wanted to send one to Grant, and ask for an explanation. Did something happen at the farm? Did he get injured?" She looks at Carolyn. "He loves you, Carolyn. Something very urgent must have come up. I must find out." Grandmother Marilyn followed her daughter out of the bedroom. She is a wider version of her daughter, but on the same small frame. They both have smiling eyes, and small bow shaped lips.

Carolyn is pacing the small cabin's floor. "I don't understand. We have had this planned for months! Why wouldn't he, at least, tell me why?" She is pacing up and down. She has her hands up in her hair, and is taking out all the pins, while walking. "I don't like my hair like this, did you, Margie? I wish I had a better style. But what difference will it make? I don't have a date for the Ball or the ceremony!" With her long auburn hair now all in disarray, she puts her head upside down, shakes it all about, and runs her fingers through it. She flips her head back up, pulls it behind her, and puts it in a simple braid. "Grant says he loves my long red hair – I want to cut it all off! That will fix him! IF HE comes to wed me – I will have hair shorter than his. I am so MAD!"

Mary goes to the red-haired firecracker. "There just has to be a logical explanation, I am sure of it. This is so unlike Grant to go back on his word or not explain things. Margie, could you go catch up with the Messenger? I must telegram Grant."

11

"Mother Mary, he knows you are here.  He would have sent you an explanation.  He is being vague on purpose, I know it!  You are wasting your time."  Carolyn stops Marjorie at the door.  "Don't waste your time, either, sister."

"I wouldn't be wasting my time.  I'd love to catch up to Richard, and bring him back.  He said that he will go to the Ball, if I am going."  She grabs her shawl to leave.

Grandmother Marilyn stops her.  "Marjorie, is that all you had on, when you came?  It is freezing out.  You'll catch your death of cold.  It is starting to snow hard out there.  Take my overcoat, please."  Margie, takes the long coat from her grandmother, and flies out the door.

Carolyn is staring at the door after it is closed.  "How could she think of going to the Ball after that telegram?  I must go home, and tell Mother the wedding is off!  No explanation, just off!"

Mary says, "Carolyn, he says he is delayed, not cancelling anything.  Let's find out what is going on before you start UN-planning your wedding.  Okay?"  She turns to her face someone level-headed.  "Mother, if Marjorie doesn't catch that young man, I will need Father Clyde to take me into town before the telegraph office closes.  Oh, what a pickle!"  She says while wringing her hands.

# THREE

## Saturday, December 2nd, 1882 in Lawrence, Kansas

The six-foot-six Colonel with dark hair and full beard is dressed in his black tie and new tails. He is patiently waiting for his wife, Julia, to finish her hair. "Julia, as hosts, we need to be there first. How much longer, my love?" He doesn't mind being late, as much as possibly missing the first dance. He loves holding his wife on the dance floor. *If only she'd stop doing her hair!*

"Will, I am almost done. Go hitch the horses or something, please. You are making me nervous!" Julia calls out to him.

"The carriage awaits, my dear." He is tired of calling to her from the living room of their little house, and goes to their bedroom door. She is still sitting at her dressing table with a comb in her hand. "Now my dear, as much as I've always said, I loved your hair piled atop your head, I never knew how much effort it took to get it there!"

"That is the trouble with marriage. All our womanly secrets come out. There, my husband, I am satisfied. Does it look okay to you?" She turns to faces him. Her dark long hair is in an up-do, but she has so much of it that she has many perfectly coiffured rolls on top with lots of curly tendrils cascading down. She also has her signature straw flowers placed throughout.

The Colonel smiles. *How can someone so beautiful - love me?* He walks over to her. "It was worth the wait. Now give us a kiss, and let's be off!"

He moves toward her, and she awkwardly moves toward him. She just recently lost a child. This was their third loss. As he sees her struggle to move, he stops. "Are you sure you are up to this? I don't want to put a strain on you so soon."

"I feel fine. It's been two weeks already. Doctor Lizzie has said that I am good to resume all normal activities." The doctor to whom she is referring is the Colonel's older sister Dr. Lizbet Lewis who is a women's doctor in Wichita. She has been Julia's physician since she was a very ill newlywed in 1879.

The Colonel shakes his head. "I know, darling, *but* if anything should happen to you, I would never forgive myself. I think that we should hold off trying to have a little one for a year or two. Let's let you build up your strength, my dear." He goes to her, now. "As much as I love dancing all night with my favorite girl, may-haps we should sit at a table for most of the songs. There will be plenty more dances to come. I promise."

She smiles at him. "And you are so good in keeping your promises." She reaches up to caress his face. "You look so very handsome in your new tails, Colonel." She adds breathlessly. "Take me dancing, please?"

He melts with her soft pleading. "How can I ever say no? I am doomed! My heart was kidnapped at seven years old, and it is still being held hostage. Luckiest Man Alive!" He kisses her cheek, leads her out of the room, and helps her put on her long wrap. It is a very cold December, so he has hired a closed carriage for the event. She is surprised by this.

"Will, you need to stop all these extravagant expenses. Our old buggy would have been fine." She says as he is helping her up the steps of the carriage.

"We need to pick up my family. I wanted us all to get there unfrozen, my love. It has been snowing since yesterday and the temperature has fallen beyond what we are accustomed to this early in the season. The cost is but a trifle compared to frozen unhappy siblings. Though the heat my infuriated sister Carolyn will emote - should keep us all warm all evening." He looks to his wife. "What could be going on with your brother Grant? He has never disappointed her before. In the three years that they have been courting, this is very unusual behavior."

He taps on the ceiling of the carriage with his walking stick to signal the hired man to start the trip. "Do you think Chilly and I should go to see if he is all right or needs help? I think if my sister doesn't get married on the Eve of Christmas Eve – Grant will need plenty of help -- then!" He says with a chuckle, but is very concerned for both his sister and Grant.

Julia looks at her childhood sweetheart. He has a 'don't-tread-on-me' attitude that served him so well in the Kansas-Cheyenne war, but everyone who knows the Colonel; knows he has the biggest heart to match his large frame. "Will,

**14**

I think that would be a good idea. He didn't answer Mother's telegram. I am also getting worried. But, couldn't your father and Chilly do it? I don't want you to go. I a . . ." She doesn't finish her thought.

"Father is getting on in years; I wouldn't want to burden him. I would have you at my Mother's home, and I wouldn't be more than two weeks or three, my darling. If Grant needs help, I need to be the one to help him. I can't imagine what could be wrong, but it must be bad if he is postponing the wedding! He has been patiently waiting for Carolyn to come of age, and get our parents' permission for their union for years." The Colonel is holding Julia's hand. "I would not forgive myself if there was something I could do, but I failed to do it. I just have this feeling something dire has happened. I am sorry, my darling. I do not want to get you upset, but truth be told, it is what I feel." He kisses the back of her hand.

Julia removes her hand from his, and caresses his face, again. "Then, I will be in good hands with Mother Beth while my brother Grant is in good hands with you. You should leave early tomorrow, for I do not want to be without you for long. Remember your promise to me. No more campaigns, no more missions. I have waited for you too long, to go through this again."

"I remember my promise, darling. If Grant is just having cold feet, I will turn around and head back the same day. I hope it is that, and nothing more serious. Now, no more discussion on this. We are at Mother's." He looks out the carriage window and sighs. "They are all waiting for us, in the dark and cold." He hastily steps out of the carriage. "Mother, why are you out here, in this freezing weather? Do you want to catch your death from cold? Come get in, all of you, get in!"

His mother, Elizabeth Palmer Lewis, is a lovely woman at fifty-four years old. She still has her slim figure, even though she bore eight babies. Her dark brown hair has a striking gray streak at her left temple. She wears her hair parted at that temple and pulled into a bun at her nape. Her husband, William Sr. is fifty-seven, and is an older version of Will, but he has gained some weight, as his father Clyde had at this same stage of life. They both take their seats in the carriage. Next to get in is Marjorie. She has dark wavy hair like Will's, but of course, it is long. She has it up in an up-do, as does Carolyn. Carolyn and Chilly are the red-heads of the family. Their coloring comes from Carolyn's namesake and maternal grandmother. She used to kid her baby brother, Charles Palmer Lewis that he was copying her. Her father laughed, and said they were as different as fire and ice. Carolyn started to call him Chilly Charlie. Everyone else did too, and soon they dropped the Charlie altogether.

Chilly is the youngest of the eight siblings. Ian was the oldest, born in 1849. He died in 1878 at the hand of Cheyenne Indians in Oberlin, Kansas. Joseph is two years younger. He is a doctor. He and Lizzie opened a practice together in Wichita, where they went to Medical school. Lizzie is two years younger than Joseph, but five years older than Will. Doomed baby Clara was barely an hour old when she was murdered by one of Quantrill's men in the Lawrence Massacre of 1863. Marjorie came the next year, then Carolyn and finally Chilly. The last four were all born a year or so from each other.

Chilly is the last to get in the carriage. He has to sit on the floor. He doesn't like it much for his new tails are getting scrunched. He doesn't complain; it is much warmer than their buggy would be.

Marjorie is all excited for the ball. She hardly slept for all she could think about was Richard Long. When she caught up to him yesterday, he was more than happy to come back to the house to help. He assured Mrs. Johnson that he would send the telegram himself. Marjorie said, "You can do that? You know how?" Then she blushed at her own awkwardness.

Richard was proud of the fact, and didn't notice her embarrassment. "I've apprenticed with Mr. Worthy for two years now. I can run the whole office, and have, several times. I will get to this right away. I will stay at the office for a response, Mrs. Johnson. I promise." He turned back to Marjorie. "Miss Lewis, I will see you tomorrow at the ball. That is a promise, too." Then he blushed, and hurried on his mission.

Mrs. Johnson looked at Margie, "I think that young man is very taken with you, my dear." Carolyn gives an exasperated noise in the background.

"He'd better come back with an answer from Grant if he

**16**

wants to dance with a Lewis girl!"

Margie just looks at her baby sister like she has two heads. "I will dance with whomever I please. It wouldn't be Richard's fault if Grant doesn't answer. Really, Carolyn, as tall as you are, sometimes you act like such a child!" With that, the tallest of the Lewis women, Carolyn, puts on her coat, and storms out the door to go home to cry on her mother's shoulder. Marjorie look at Grandmother Marilyn and her daughter Mary. "Well, she does!"

\*\*\*

The Ball is such a success! Colonel William Lewis and his Julia are known for holding these Grand Balls, from EL Dorado to Leavenworth. The Colonel does not let his wife dance too often, much to her disappointment, as well as his own. Marjorie and her new young beau make up for them. Marjorie is the same height as her mother, just barely five feet. Richard Long was shorter than all the Lewis men, but still much taller than Marjorie. They make a lovely couple on the dance floor.

Carolyn dances all night, but not with the same young man twice. She pretends to have a great time, but the family knows that she is putting on a very brave face. She is missing her Grant, so very much. She smiles at the fella holding her, and pretends to listen to what he is saying, but she doesn't hear a word. Her mind is thinking a thousand thoughts at once. She has no doubt that Grant loves her. *He was so happy when my parents finally agreed to the marriage. He even had happy tears fall from his eyes! He must be in trouble. I should go to him to see if he is alright.* She knew that he wouldn't answer his mother's telegram. She knows something is wrong. But here she is dancing as if she doesn't have a care in the world, and hating every minute of it!

At one point during the evening, Will pulls his father to the side to tell him of his thought to go to EL Dorado to see if Grant needs help. He asks if Chilly can accompany him. His father just laughs, and says, "Try to stop him!"

Chilly and Will had gone on an Indian adventure two years prior. Chilly, now almost six-foot-eight, and still growing, was only 14 years old at the time, but almost Will's height. They

**17**

had heard that their brother Ian's son, Joshua, had survived the Cheyenne massacre in Oberlin. He was captured by them, and taken to Wyoming. They had crossed several states in search for their nephew. There was no need to get justice for Joshua because his mother also survived, and they were at home with their new Cheyenne life. It was with great sadness that they left them both in Wyoming. Back in Lawrence, though, Chilly has not been content with school and the farmer's life. He still longs for adventure, and insists that he will join the cavalry like Will, the older brother with whom he shares a birthday.

# FOUR

## Saturday Dec 2nd, 1882 in EL Dorado

Grant wakes before sunrise. He had a very restless night. He received the telegram from his mother, but there was nothing that he could tell her yet. He knows that Carolyn was looking forward to the Ball, and their dancing together. He always went to Lawrence for the Balls that the Colonel hosted. It was a great excuse to hold his love and dance with her, since that was all he allowed himself to do. He has been in love with her since 1879, but she was only fourteen and he was twenty-four. She was wild, silly, happy – a true firecracker, and a breath of fresh air. His sister, Julia, had brought her to visit EL Dorado for a few weeks, and she captivated his attention, first, with that wonderful long red hair, then the way she carried herself at such a young age. *Now, he was breaking her heart! Will she ever forgive me?*

He gets up and dresses. He can smell Annabelle's coffee. He is nothing before coffee. He is going to meet his Uncle Ben in town. He needs to have his wits about him.

A few days ago, he had run into his father's half-brother, the oldest one, at the Feed store in town. Ben had talked him into going for a drink. During that talk, his uncle told him some very disturbing news. It seems that Ben had heard two rumors, and was very eager to spread them. Grant did not want to believe either of them, but the more that he thought about them, the more they festered and embedded themselves.

Ben had word about one of the young negro girls that worked at the Farm at the time Grant moved in. She now has a mulatto child about five years old. Ben told Grant that he has her hidden away, but she was willing to come forward to admit that her child was Grant's! Grant told him that it wasn't possible, but Ben reminded him of the New Year's Eve party that Grant attended, and had too much to drink. Grant was so drunk that Ben brought him home. Ben said that Molly was the one that helped put Grant to bed that night. Molly told Ben that Grant did not sleep alone. When she found out that she was with child, she ran away. Grant laughed at the

**19**

ridiculousness of the story, but now that he has had time to think about it . . .

Ben had other disturbing news as well. It was this news that had Grant heart-broken and shaken. Ben said he had proof on its way, and Grant demanded to see it. They agreed to meet today. Ben had told Grant that he can make both problems disappear -- for the right sum.

That is the problem. The right sum is more than Grant is willing to pay. Ben wants Grant to give up the rights to the Farmhouse, and the estate that goes with it. Grant loves the farm, and working the land. He has increased his holdings by fifty percent, in the six years since he inherited it. But if either of these rumors get out – he could be ruined. He must see proof before he'd even consider it.

It is another bitter cold day. Grant is in town at one p.m. They meet in the hotel restaurant. They are seated in the back of the room and they both order coffee, but do not exchange any pleasantries. Though the tension between them was thick, to the casual passers-by they looked very much alike; same color brown eyes, same hair color and set jawline. Grant was just a taller, thinner version of his uncle.

Grant impatiently asks, "What proof do you have? These are huge lies, and I won't believe them until I see the proof for myself!"

"You said as much, but once you see it, you'll believe. I have a letter from her to her lover admitting to the affair, and claiming that the bastard child is his. I just received the letter, this morning. I have paid very handsomely for it."

"Let me see it! I will know her handwriting. Why would she . . ." Ben hands him the much-folded dirty letter. The letter looks decades old. Grant reads it. He turns it over, and looks at the back. Then he rereads the front again.

"Well? Do you believe me now?" Ben, shorter than Grant by three inches, goes to take the letter away, but Grant is too fast for him.

"Is this the only proof that you have?" He starts to tear up the letter. He gets only a corner ripped, when someone behind him grabs his arms to stop him.

"I assumed you'd try to do that. I came prepared. Meet my man Thornton." While the taller Thornton has both of

Grant's arms pinned, Ben takes the paper from Grant's hand, very carefully. "You'll have to do better than that, Grant." Thornton lets go of Grants arms, but puts pressure on his shoulders to make him sit, again.

"This isn't even close to her handwriting!" He says loudly, and the folks in the restaurant look up.

Ben looks uncomfortable with people staring. "Why don't you ask her yourself? I am sure she will admit it. What else can she do? You'll know by the look on her face if she tries to lie. You know her all too well to be fooled." Ben pauses for affect. "Again, I mean." He gives a chuckle. "There is still the matter of Molly. I think her son would like to meet his father. What would you have given to know your real father, when you were five?" He chuckles again. "That's a trick question, isn't it? Since Steven wasn't your real father, or so it says in your MOTHER'S letter!"

Grant stands up. "Don't you dare say that! You have no real proof. If you did, you would have hired an attorney, and have the will contested, since you'd be the true heir to the estate if Steven had no male issue. I am done with this and ALL conversations. Do not contact me again!"

Grant puts a few coins on the table for the coffee he never touched, and walks out without looking back. *The nerve of him, with that damn forged letter! And here I sent that telegram for this. I hope Carolyn will forgive me.*

"Grant!" Ben calls to Grant's back. "We are not through here, I assure you. Now that I have the letter in my hands, I WILL go to my attorneys. Just know - I will not stop until I have back MY family plantation. I promise!

*That sounds more like a weak threat,* Grant thinks as he keeps walking.

# FIVE

## Sunday, December 3rd, 1882 in Lawrence

Carolyn is awake before daybreak, even though they all had a late night at the Ball. She needs to know what is delaying her fiancé. Will is going to EL Dorado with Chilly this morning, to make sure Grant is all right. Carolyn figures that she has a right to be there, too. She knows that no one will allow it, but she is determined.

Julia and Will are at the house at seven-thirty in the morning to pick up Chilly. Carolyn is the first out of the house to greet her older brother. He looks tired after the events of last night. "Good morning, sister. I don't want you to worry about Grant. I promised my bride that I will help him with anything that could be delaying him." He is helping Julia down from the buckboard. With his hands on her tiny waist, he easily lifts her up, and swings her around. "Luckiest man alive!" He says, quietly, in her ear, and he puts her down. Julia blushes.

Carolyn smiles. "You two are really something. Married three years, and you act as if it still the first week. Please hurry and help my Grant, so that I can have that, too!"

Julia goes to her, puts her arm around Carolyn's waist, and says, "If anyone can help, it will be the Colonel! I will be staying here with you and your family, while he and Chilly go to EL Dorado. Can you get my bag?" Will has already taken it down from the back of the buckboard, and starts to hand it to Carolyn. She is too preoccupied to notice.

"Is Chilly ready to go?" He asks.

"I don't know. Why don't you take your wife in the house? I was on my way to the barn, to get eggs for Mother. I will be done in just a few minutes." Julia and Will head toward the house, and Carolyn acts as if she is going to the barn.

The homestead was built by Clyde and William for the newlyweds thirty-six years ago. They have added on bedrooms and modernized the kitchen as the family grew. In preparation for the wedding, William Sr. and his sons put up new clapboards and painted. It is one of the biggest farmhouses in the county.

As the couple enter the house, The Colonel calls, "Good morning, everyone. Chilly, are you ready? I'd like to get lots of miles in today." Everyone in the house answers at once.

"Good morning, I hope you have a safe trip. Mary is so worried," says Will's mother.

"What a wonderful ball you hosted last night, brother. I had the best time! The band was magnificent! I could have danced all night!" Marjorie is at Julia's side. "Good morning, dear sister. How are you this wonderful morning?" She gives Julia a kiss.

His father says, "I should go with you. I don't like this at all."

Chilly says, "I am ready, brother. Let's get on the road!"

Julia and the Colonel laugh. They could not tell who was saying what, with everyone talking at once.

Since Chilly is set to go, he and the Colonel waste no time in loading up the buckboard with the extra provisions that his mother insists they need. "That looks like everything. I will send a telegram as soon as I know what is going on. Where is Carolyn? I wanted to assure her that I will do my best to get her groom to town for her Eve of Christmas Eve wedding." He calls out toward the barn. "Carolyn, we are leaving. Come wish us luck." He waits for a few moments, but there is no reply from Carolyn. "I think we should go. Carolyn must have lost track of time. Julia, keep an eye on her for me, please? I'll watch your sibling if you watch mine." He gives her a wink and chuckles. He kisses her on the cheek and gets up into the buckboard. Again, everyone speaks at once to say good-bye. Will stands in the buckboard to look toward the barn, one last time, then gives a flick to the reins, and he and Chilly start their journey. He wants to get to Ottawa by eleven so they can attend Sunday service.

Two hours later, they pull off the road just before Ottawa to eat a little something before going into town for the services. Chilly jumps down, and goes to the back of the buckboard for the bag of sandwiches. When he goes to lift the bag, Carolyn sits up and says, "It is about time you stopped. I thought I would go crazy waiting under that blanket. How far are we?"

The Colonel answers. "I had a feeling that you were hiding back there. The Carolyn that I know would have given us a thousand instructions before we left town. Getting eggs was an awful excuse. I even told Father that I would send a telegram at the first town to confirm your presence. We will do that here in Ottawa, after church service."

"He didn't want to stop me?" She is surprised.

"As much as you do not want to admit it, Carolyn, you are more like myself and Chilly. You lead with your heart, not your head. Though you have one of those, also. In time, the head will take charge. I knew that you couldn't sit idly by while *I* investigate your future. Come up front, and have a sandwich. Did you bring any extra clothing with you?" He looks in the buckboard, and doesn't see anything extra in it.

"I didn't want to risk detection. I assumed I could buy some things in EL Dorado before or after we get to the Farmhouse. I did bring my coin purse. The most important thing is to find out why Grant is delayed, and clear it up!" She climbs into the front of the buckboard, and sits sandwiched by her tall brothers. "We just have to keep our wedding date of the Eve of Christmas Eve."

"We will do what we can, Carolyn. You might have to be a little flexible on that date, though."

"Never! It is all planned down to the smallest detail." She says as she takes a petite bite out of her sandwich. "No, we must keep that date!!" She adds. The Colonel gives a small laugh, and gives a flick of the reins to start the horses.

# SIX

## Monday, December 4th, 1882 in EL Dorado

Grant is awake before sun-up. He is going to town to see his lawyers. He is sure that the letter is a fake, but he must prepare them for a fight. He is at a lost for a plan. He is not worried about the Molly situation. He is sure that even in a drunken state, he would not take advantage of a girl that way. Though, she did leave suddenly that March, after weeks of ill humor. He remembers that vividly. She was a sweet-natured girl before that. She must have been with child. Just not his!

When he goes into the dining room, little Matilda is setting the table. "Mattie, can you get your mother? I need to talk with her." He sits at the head, and waits for Annabelle to come. She enters the room, quickly, with a large spoon still in her hand.

"Master Grant, how can I serve you?" She does a curtsey.

"I have told you many times, Annie, I do not like to be called Master, my father fought a war to stop the Master/Slave thing, and you have been a free woman since before I was born."

"You iz still the Master of this here estate, and I'z will call you the title you deserve. Now, what can I do for you, sir?"

"Annabelle, can I be honest with you?" He pulls out a seat at the table for her to sit. When he points to it, she shakes her head no, and takes a step backward. "I insist." He adds.

"Sir, iz I gonna be fired?"

Grant gives an honest chuckle. "Annie, I will make you stand, if I fire you. Now sit!" She finally does, puts the spoon on the table, and turns to her employer.

"Start being honest, Master Grant." She claps her hand together and doesn't make eye contact.

"Okay, I have a problem, and I need your help, I think."

"You thinks *Iz* can help?" She looks up at him.

"Yes. What do you know of young Molly who was here when I first inherited?"

"She was an ungrateful child. Your father freed her, and

**25**

then died so she could stay free, but she run off like a no-account N . . . !" She doesn't finish the word. She makes a 'tsk-tsk' sound with her tongue. "She were an awful sour puss before she left. 'Member?"

"Yes, I remember. Do you have any idea what became of her? Or why she left so abruptly? I would have let her go freely, if she had come to me and asked. That is what hired people do."

Annie looks around the room to see if Matilda might be close by. She leans in close to Grant. "Oh, Iz heardz, she was wit' child. Don't know if true or not, but that iz what I'z heard. Why are you asking 'bout her, Master?"

"I heard she was back in town. She is working with my Uncle Ben to try and make trouble for me."

"Oh, he's a bad man, Master Grant. He were never nice to us, like your folks was. He were too much like your Grandfather. God rest his soul, if he had one. He were as mean as they came! That woman he married and buried were none better. Your Aunt Gloria and Uncle George are good folks, but their parents was just plain cruel."

Grant puts his hand on hers. "I am sorry that you suffered under them, Annie. I am ashamed for it. But I need your help with Molly. Is there anything you can find out about her, through your friends?"

"A-course, Master Grant, I'll see what they say over the warsh-boards 'bout her. I am sure someone has seen her or knowz her where-'bouts."

Clarence passes the dining room. He suddenly stops to stare at them. "Sir, iz thar something you need?" He is now looking at his wife casually sitting next to their young master.

Annabelle jumps up. "Never you mind, Clarence Tobias Johnson. This is nuthin' fer you to worrit 'bout. Now you get in that thar kitchen, and help me bring Master Grant's breakfast out here, while it is still hot!" She is waving her spoon at him. Grant just chuckles to himself. *Annie rules this roost, no doubt about it! Hopefully, she can get me the information I need.*

\*\*\*

Grant is on his horse Romeo, coming back from his

lawyers. His head is swimming. They were of little help. The lawyers told him that he needs to prove the letter was a fake. *How am I supposed to do that? What am I paying them for?* "Romeo, you're more help than they were. And they are going to charge me a fee, just for telling them my problem! God, I hate lawyers!" Romeo gives a snort in his way of response. "What am I going to do? Do you have any ideas?" Again, Romeo snorts, this time with an extra shake of his head. "I didn't think so. It's okay, boy, I won't hold it against you."

Grant leads Romeo into the stable. Clarence is waiting. "Sir, I will brush him down and feed him. Master, may I tell you somethin'?"

"Of course, Clarence, what is on your mind?"

"It's 'bout young Molly. Annie said you'd be askin' 'bout her. Well, I hear'd word that she brought a youngin into town. I remember before she was leavin'. She was miserable after your first New Year celebration. I 'member that I thought it was picullar how she hung on your Uncle Ben when he was around. Annie seyz that he is startin' trouble for ye. If I wuz a bettin' man, I'd say that Uncle was the pappy of that youngin'. It's just a feelin'. I ain't got no way to prove it, a-course. I thought you should know'd 'bout it, is all."

"Thank you, Clarence. That could be helpful to know. Do you know of any other relationships that my Uncle might have had with girls like young Molly?"

"Didja want a list, sir? If I'z thinks 'bout it for a while . . . I will get Annie to scribble up some names, sir. Anythin' we can do to help you, Master."

"You know that I hate being called that."

"Annie would have my hide if I didn't, sir."

"I believe that! How is Joan Of Arc? I thought she would have had that foal by now."

"She ain't on our schedule, sir."

"Tell that to my fiancée." Grant mutters as he leaves.

Clarence calls after him. "Beg pardon, Sir?

# SEVEN

## Tuesday, December 6<sup>th</sup>, 1882 in EL Dorado

"This is the longest trip! Why is this taking so long!" Carolyn complains. Her two brothers who tower over her 5'8' frame just shrug their shoulders. She has not been the best traveling companion. They understand her impatience. She is upset from worry.

"Carolyn, you need to relax a bit. Whatever is the problem, Chilly and Willie are here to fix it! This is what we do!" Chilly says with complete conviction.

The Colonel adds, "I don't know why I started that 'Chilly and Willie' phrase. I hate being called Willie. Even when I was young, I wasn't a 'wee Willie'. Now, I am Navoualevè. I have always been too big to be 'wee' anything." The Cheyenne gave him the name, which translates as 'too tall' in French, during his mission as a Major, escorting them to their Northern Ancestral home in Montana.

"I know we don't have much farther. The closer we are, the more nervous I am getting. What could possibly be the problem?" Once again, her brothers both just shrug. "Really, you guys are a lot of help!"

\*\*\*

At a little before two, they are in EL Dorado. Main Street is bustling with business. Carolyn has changed places with Chilly so she can look at the stores as they pass. "We need to stop. I don't want Grant to see me, looking like I have spent three days and nights in the same dress. I do not know what I was thinking not bringing at least one change of clothing. Can we stop at Anita's Dress Shop? They have lots of great dresses, and big dressing rooms to change in. I won't take long. I promise."

The Colonel smiles, "That's what every woman says when going to shop for a new dress! I am not in as big as rush as you are. Just take your time; it's not our fiancé that needs

**28**

help!  Right, Chilly?"

"So right, Colonel!"  He agrees.

An hour later, the trio is on its way to the Johnson Family Farms.  Carolyn bought three new dresses, and redid her hair up on top of her head.  She doesn't look like she was on the road for three minutes, let alone three days.  "See, I told you that I wouldn't be long!"

The Colonel looks at his watch then to Chilly.  "Julia would still be on the first dress.  I guess we are lucky."  Then he looks to his little sister.  "You look just gorgeous, my dear.  I know how important that is to you young ladies.  We should be at the plantation in just a bit."

"I cannot thank you enough for doing this for me, Will.  You too, Chilly.  I just hope it is something that we can help, and he doesn't have cold feet.  He has patiently waited for me to come of age.  This is not like the Grant that I know.  I am just at a loss to explain it."

"Not to worry, Carolyn, we will fix it soon enough!"  He puts his arm around her protectively.  He turns the buckboard onto the Johnson property.  "And here we are!"  They pass through the wooded drive and are soon in front of the house.

"I love this Farmhouse.  It has been in Grant's family for generations.  I cannot wait to live here."  She is trying to get down through Chilly.

Hold on, sis.  I'll get down first and help you."  By the time he gets her down, the door to the Farmhouse opens.  Seven-year-old Matilda is down the steps, and is in Carolyn's arms in seconds.

Oh, Miss Carolyn!  I iz so happy to see ya!"  She has her arms around Carolyn's waist, and is holding her tight.  "I am looking forward to you being the Mistress of the house.  I begged Maw to let me go with Master Grant for the wedding.  She won't let me!  I just want to cry for the want of goin'!  Please, can you talk wit her?  I know she will say yes, if you're a askin' her.  Please?"

"Mattie, I don't know.  I will consider it."  Carolyn is all smiles.  This little one hasn't heard that the wedding might not take place.  *That's a good sign!*  She looks up at the large home.  It is an old Colonial style, twenty-room mansion with eight bedrooms.  She laughed the first time she saw it, after she heard her sister-in-law Julia refer to it as the 'Farmhouse'. This mansion is nothing like any farmhouse she has seen.

As she is trying to walk to the front steps with Mattie still around her waist, the door opens again. Carolyn can feel herself take a breath in, that she is afraid to let out. "Oh, Grant!" She says half to herself. He is all smiles when he sees her, and runs down the steps. Mattie lets go of her waist just in time for Grant to grab her there, and swing her around.

"Carolyn, what are you doing here? You are such a sight for sore eyes! I thought you'd be too mad at me to talk to me again, let alone come here!" He swings her around, again. He puts her down, and slowly bends over to give her a kiss on her cheek, but before doing so he asks. "May I kiss you? I have missed you so much!"

"Oh, Grant. You still want me? You haven't gotten cold feet, then."

"Never my darling. I just have a few things that needed my immediate attention, before I am free to wed. I should have said more in my telegram, but I didn't know how to explain it."

Carolyn is so happy that she throws her arms around his neck. "Oh, Grant. Kiss me, Grant. Kiss me NOW!" He bends down again. He is aiming for her cheek, but she leans in to meet his lips. He is pleasantly surprised.

The Colonel and Chilly are still at the buckboard. Finally, Chilly says, "Ahem! So, what is going on, Grant?" The couple breaks apart, and they are both flushed from the embrace. "We are here to help you with whatever has delayed you. How can we help?"

"Oh, where are my manners. Annabelle has just put on a fresh pot of tea. Please come into the Farmhouse for me to explain everything. It is a very sordid story, and I hope that you believe me, that none of what he says is true."

Mattie has run back into the house. Her father, Clarence, has come out of the stable to take the reins of the buckboard. "Sirs, let me take care of your horses. Do you have bags to be brought in?" Chilly has taken his and the Colonel's carpetbags off the back of the buckboard. He hands them to Clarence. He has Carolyn's large tissue-wrapped packages from the store, and hands that to Clarence, also. "Iz will bring these in, and take good care of the animals. Such a good pair of horses, sir."

Chilly answers. "They are; they have been worked hard to get here. They need a good brush down and some oats, if you have them."

"Course, sir. Right away."

"Clarence, call me Chilly. 'Sir' is my father."

"No, sir, can't do that, but I will take care of the animals as soon as Iz bring in your bags."

Chilly gives the forty-something-year-old ex-slave a second glance. "Why can't you call me Chilly? Everyone does."

"My wife would have my hide for disrespecting my betters. We must do what Annie says, or trouble will be a-brewing!" He puts his head down, and hurries into the house. Chilly just shrugs, and follows him in.

***

With the afternoon tea poured, and fresh baked sweet cakes served, they are all at the dining room table as Grant begins to explain the embarrassing situation. "It's my Uncle Ben, he approached me with two reasons to blackmail me. I refused to pay because both of his reasons are bull . . . um . . . Sorry, Carolyn, you all know what I mean to say."

"Poppycock – in other words?" She blushes. She has never been so direct.

"Exactly, but my nonpayment might not be the end of my problems. Ben is insisting that he will go to his lawyers to force my hand. My lawyers told me I need to find proof that the letter is forged. I hate lawyers."

The Colonel interrupts, "Grant, start at the beginning – what is he alleging?"

"Yes, where to begin? First off, he is claiming that I took advantage of one of our house negroes during my first New Year's Eve here. He is claiming that the girl has given birth to my son. It is not true! Even as drunk as I was, I would have not have done what he is accusing me of." He is looking at Carolyn, during the whole story. "You do believe me, don't you, my dear? I will die if you don't believe me." He seems to be holding his breath.

She reaches across the table to grab his hand. "Of course, I believe you. What kind of a wife would I be, if I didn't back you up. I would believe you, if you said you were Santa Claus, and you swore to me it was true!"

Grant lets out his breath. He jumps up, goes to her side of the table, and kneels next to her chair. "I was so afraid that you'd be upset, and not want anything to do with me, anymore." He hangs his head down.

She reaches out to him, lifts his head to see a tear escape his right eye, and one about to fall from his left. "Oh, my darling. I love you. Did you think I am so shallow as to pass judgement on you, so easily? Or not believe you? I am almost hurt. I know you think I am very young, but I have more sense than that." She kisses his cheek. "Now, tell us the second blackmail part."

"The next one might be more serious, and it's not my secret to tell." He kisses her cheek and stands. He walks back to his chair and sits. "But you are all family, and I am sure that Mother won't mind, since you came to help."

He is silent, once again. He is struggling to form his sentences. "Uncle says he has written proof in my Mother's handwriting that I am not Stephen Johnson's son. Therefore, I am not heir to the Johnson Family Farm Estate. I saw the letter he claimed was hers for just a minute. It was written to the 'other man,' and the writer said that she was going to leave her husband to marry the real father of her little boy. The paper looked old enough, and the handwriting looked somewhat like Mother's, but there is no way to know for sure – other than this is *my mother we are talking about!* It is beyond impossible that she would ever have a lover, let alone want to leave Father for him. She has told so many loving stories about Father. I know she truly loved him. I remember when she got the news that he died in battle. She took to her bed, and wept for three days. I remember my heartless Step-Grandmother yelling at her to stop being lazy, and get over 'it'. My mother still has not gotten over 'it', after all these years without him." He pauses to look at all their faces. "I could lose the farm if he takes me to court over this."

Carolyn is the first to speak. "Grant, I don't believe it either. Even if your uncle gets the courts to believe it, and you lose everything, I will still love you, and want to be your wife. You can come to Lawrence to help run our plantation. Right,

**32**

Will?"

"He would be a wonderful addition to Legacy Plantation. But that is the last resort; let's save HIS farm, if we can."

Chilly looks to his older brother. "Legacy Plantation? When did we start calling it that?"

"Just now. I just thought of Mom's oval samplers that said The Lewis Legacy, and thought that our farm should be called something special."

"I like it. Now, how do we save the Johnson Family Farms?" Carolyn asks.

"That might take a little more thought." The Colonel says. "I think we need more information about your uncle's comings and goings, for starters."

# EIGHT

## Thursday, December 8th, 1882 in EL Dorado

The last two days were spent trying to get information about Molly and Uncle Ben. Clarence drove Chilly and the Colonel to a few bars, so they could buddy up to any customers that might know Benjamin Johnson.

He also took Annabelle to town to shop, and see what she can find out about Molly. None of these queries led to any answers.

The Colonel, in his desperation, even wired a retired Army friend of his to see if he could be of assistance. This friend also worked for Allan Pinkerton in the Pinkerton National Detective Agency. Truly, he has the experience to offer suggestions, at least, Will thought.

Today, Carolyn is in town to buy more dresses. Grant drove her in, himself. He is in the store waiting for her to show him the dress that he picked out for her.

"I love this!" Carolyn says as she rushes out of the dressing room. The color is teal and the skirt is very full. "This dress I can wear at the Colonel's Easter Ball. What do you think, my dear?"

"I think that you are beyond beautiful in it. Do you have to wait until Spring to wear it?"

"Think of it this way. By then you'll be able to help me out of it!" As soon as she says this she blushes redder than her hair.

"That is exactly what I was thinking." He is blushing also. "I cannot wait until we are husband and wife so I could have that honor. He takes her by the waist, and lifts her up to give her a little swing.

"Only two weeks left, Grant." She says smiling in his arms.

He puts her down, and leans in. "I don't think I can wait two days. I want you so bad."

"Oh, Grant. You behave yourself! Do I have to have one of my brothers sleep outside my room to keep my honor safe, until then?" She lovingly gives him a swat on the shoulder.

"I think that you might have to, knowing you are just down the hall from me might be too much temptation for me. Though, I only go where I am invited. You only have to say the word, and I will pay you a midnight visit."

"As much as I would love to, my Darling, I am going to keep myself pure for my rightful husband. What if I give myself to you, and you decide not to walk me down the aisle? I would be disgraced!"

"I would never do that to you."

"I never thought you'd send that telegram, either. I am just saying that I need to protect my own honor since I am the one who must live with the consequences. Now, do I need set an armed guard outside my door? Or are you going to behave?"

"I will behave until you tell me otherwise."

She gives him a kiss on his cheek. "That is the correct answer, my love. Now, that pink dress has caught my eye. What do you think of that one?"

"It doesn't do anything for your fair complexion or your beautiful red hair. That dress would be perfect on my sister Julia, though. We should get it for her, and see if Will approves."

"That is a wonderful idea. We should buy all my siblings something for Christmas. Shall we? Do you mind?"

"Go right ahead. If this is my last year as the Master of the estate, I might as well go out with a bang."

Carolyn stops in place with two dresses in her hands. "Nothing like that is going to happen. We will fight this! I think we need to have a serious talk with your mother. I agree that it doesn't seem like Mother Mary, but everyone is young and stupid once."

"Except you, my dear. Our discussion, just now, proves you are virtuous. It can be done if one has a mind to do it."

She rushes to him, and leans in to say. "I have not said no lightly. I dream every night about what our married life will be like." She looks around, then says, "Especially the marriage bed part!" She is blushing again. She fans herself and adds, "I need to get out of this dress. I have only found these two dresses that I would like to try on. Do you like them?"

"I am sorry, my girl. My mind was still picturing what you said were your dreams. What else did you say?"

"Never mind, I am going into the dressing room," she says as she shakes her head. As she walks away, she says under her breath, *"Oh, Grant, I cannot wait to have you, either!"*

\*\*\*

The evening meal is served at 6 p.m. Carolyn is dressed in one of the dresses that Grant picked out. The Colonel and Chilly had heard some news from town. Annabelle, Clarence and even little Matilda served dinner, and the family ate heartily. Finally, Carolyn says, "Will, what have you found out?"

"I heard that Ben was trying to find a forger. He was willing to pay handsomely for a handwritten document."

"They used that word 'handsomely'? Exactly?" Grant asks with his mouth agape.

"Yes, that was the very word, why?" The Colonel replied.

"Ben admitted that he paid 'handsomely' for the letter. I think we are on to something. Do you know who he used?"

"No, but I plan to find out. I am going back to the bar tonight. This guy Lucas said that he will get back to me. He knows a guy that may have helped him, and if I am willing to grease the wheels, I may get what I need tonight!"

Annabelle comes in, and goes to Grant with a piece of paper. He looks at the note, then at her, "Are you sure about this, Annie?"

"Oh, yessum, Master Grant. I talked wit' several folks who has seen the goin's on there. I swear." She does a curtsey, and retreats into the kitchen.

"Will, I think that we have a small trip that we need to make together." He hands the Colonel the note.

Carolyn interrupts. "Is it safe? I don't want any of my menfolk in harm's way. Even tonight, Will, please be safe."

"Carolyn, I was in a war. I can take care of myself and others." He chuckles. "Tell you what, I will bring Chilly with me for protection."

"Willie and Chilly together will be unbeatable! Sorry, Colonel, I know how you hate that saying."

"Only from the moment it left my lips!" Will grumbled. They all laugh.

***

After Will and Chilly go back to the bar to meet with Lucas, the house is quiet. Grant and Carolyn retire to their beds.

Hours later, a door opens in the dark of night. Carolyn cannot sleep. She has a candle in hand lighting the way. She goes downstairs, starts to head to the kitchen for a drink, but changes her mind, and goes to the front door. She opens it, and sees that a light snow is falling. Kansas doesn't get much snow and for it to fall before the Holidays seems magical. She closes the door for a second.

She puts her candle on the foyer table and grabs the white fox fur gloves and stole that Grant bought her during their recent shopping spree, and puts it around her shoulders and goes out onto the porch. *I need to be honest with Grant,* she thinks. She steps down off the porch and walks down the wooded driveway until she can see the moon between the trees. It seems to give her the strength she needs. She breaths in the crisp air. The snow is wetting her hair, which is down and unbraided, the dampness is bringing out all her natural curls. *I need to do it now, before I lose my nerve.* She goes back into the house as quietly as she can.

She tiptoes back up the stairs as her single candle's light leads the way down the narrow hallway. Carolyn is holding her breath. She thinks that the beating of her heart is making enough noise to be heard downstairs in the servants' room. She stands outside of Grant's door, and raises her arm to knock. Her nerves overcome her, and she freezes with her arm still in mid-air. *Do I dare? What if . . .* Her mind doesn't finish the thought, because she hears movement on the other side of the door.

She turns to flee back down the hall when she hears, "Carolyn? What are you doing up? I thought you had retired for the night."

She shyly turns around. "Grant, can we talk? Downstairs?" He nods consent then takes her arm, and leads her back to the stairway.

"Carolyn, you are cold and wet. Were you outside?"

"Yes. I couldn't sleep and thought the crisp air would

clear my head. It is snowing." She is in her new white dressing gown and he is in his robe. Her hair is dripping on the gown, and she is nervously twists some of it with the hand not holding the candle. She lets go of her hair, and her whole body is trembles as she reaches for the stair railing.

When they get to the still lit front parlor, she blows out her candle, and turns to him. She blushes, and looks down. "Grant, I am very . . . nervous to bring this up."

"What is it? We're alone, you can tell me anything." He reaches for her. She sidesteps his embrace. "Are you mad at me, Carolyn?"

"I am . . . concerned. I understand that you were worried about your Uncle Ben, but I am not sure why that stopped you from coming to Lawrence?"

"Ben said that he would have the proof for me on Saturday. I had to see what he had to show me. I didn't know where that would lead so I wired on the side of caution that I would be delayed two or three weeks."

"That was all? The meeting with your Uncle on Saturday? Nothing else?" She goes to him, and fixes the turned under collar of his robe. "I was so worried that you waited for me too long, and that you changed your mind."

"I explained it all to you when you came. Didn't you believe me?" He reaches for her hands. "Your hands are so cold." He brings them both to his lips.

"I did . . . I do . . . but a girl can get a little insecure."

"Carolyn, I have never met a girl as confident as you. Is it all an act?" He kisses the back of her hands, again.

She removes he hands from his, pausing to choose her words, carefully. "Deep down, I am afraid that you are using this as a convenient ruse to delay or back out of our wedding. If you are getting cold feet, tell me now, and I will go back to Lawrence. Heartbroken, but with my head held high."

"Don't ever leave me, Carolyn. I will marry you tomorrow. We can go to Reverend Scott and get married quietly, then go to Lawrence for the big event, if you want. Two weddings should convince you of my love."

"You would do that? Marry me tomorrow?"

"I will send Clarence to town for Reverend Scott tonight, if you prefer. Marry me in that dressing gown. Then I can take it off you!"

"Oh, Grant!" She puts her head on his shoulder as her burdensome unease is lifted. She looks up, and gives him a chaste kiss on the lips. She backs out of his arms, and grasps her hands as if in a prayer and puts them thoughtfully to her lips. She is silent for a moment, then smiles shyly. "Yes! Send Clarence, tonight! I do not want to waste another moment being Miss Lewis. I want to be your legal wife, tonight!"

Grant is shocked at her acceptance of his proposal. He looks at the clock on the fireplace mantel. It is after eleven. "I was going to wait up for your brothers. They should be home soon from the meet with that Lucas fellow at the bar. We will need them as witnesses to make it official. Are you sure, Carolyn? You do not want to wait for your Eve of Christmas Eve wedding day?"

Carolyn scoffs. "Oh, I will not be cheated out of the big wedding that all of Lawrence is going to attend! But if we marry tonight, I won't have the nervousness of our first night together to worry about."

"So you want to marry me tonight to calm your nerves? I feel used!"

"I think, if you go wake up Clarence, and get him on the road for that preacher, you will have a chance to feel 'used' before morning!" She blushes past her red hair color, once again. "I cannot believe that I just said that!"

Before Grant can answer her, Will and Chilly come in the front doors, brushing the new fallen snow off of themselves.

The brothers stop in their tracks to look at Grant and Carolyn both blushing from their conversation, and standing in the parlor in their night clothes. The Colonel is the first to speak. "Is there something going on, we should know about?"

Grant answers him. "Carolyn has just agreed to marry me. Isn't that great!" Without further explanation, Grant starts to walk to the servants' quarters.

The Colonel looks at Carolyn, "I thought you said yes to his proposal months ago. That is why we are here, to make sure he gets to Lawrence for the wedding."

Carolyn is still blushing red. "He is going to get Clarence to wake up the preacher to marry us TONIGHT!"

"What about the Eve of Christmas Eve?" asks her

**39**

younger brother.

"We are going to get married then, too. Isn't it wonderful?"

Chilly looks to Will. "Am I missing something? Why do they need to get married twice? It doesn't make a bit of sense."

The Colonel goes to his little sister, and gives her a hug. "I think it is just grand, Sis." He looks to Chilly. "When you are in love, Chilly, it does not have to make a bit of sense to anyone, but them. I suppose we are to stay awake for these nuptials?"

"Yes, we need you as a witness!" She is smiling from ear to ear. "You too, Chilly. We need two witnesses."

Chilly looks to his brother, again. "Is she getting married like that? Is her hair wet?"

"Yes, I was outside for a moment. I wanted to see the snowfall. It is magical."

"Go put on the teal ball gown you were telling me about, Carolyn. Chilly and I will change into our Sunday clothes."

Grant comes back into the room. "I am going to put on my tie and tails. When I woke Clarence to ask him to go to town, Annie thought you needed a doctor or something. When I told her that we were getting married, I swear she turned as white as you and me!" He stepped forward to take his fiancée's hand. "Shall we dress for our wedding, my love?" They head up the staircase hand in hand.

Chilly starts to snicker. Then, he sashays over to Will, and takes his hand. "Shall we dress for their wedding, dear brother?" The Colonel tries to hold back the laughter as he and Chilly sashay up the stairs still hand in hand, just like the soon-to-be bride and groom.

# NINE

## Friday, December 8<sup>th</sup>, 1882 in EL Dorado

Clarence did not dally in his mission. He was back with Reverend Scott in a little more than an hour's time. Carolyn had used every second of it to make herself ready. She has her hair up in fancy rolls high on her head. Annie helped her put on the exquisite teal ball gown. It had a low neckline and a very tight bodice. There was white lace covering her womanly charms, and white lace as the underskirt that showed where the teal silk is gathered up in bows. The bustle was much smaller as is the new fashion, but the bottom of the skirt is much fuller and moves easily back and forth in a swaying motion.

While Carolyn is getting prepped and ready. Will is filling Grant in on the meeting with Lucas. "I offered to double whatever Ben paid for his forged letter for a similar letter in the same handwriting and aged look. This way Ben's letter would not stand up in court as authentic, when they are compared side by side."

Grant was astonished. "Colonel, that is a brilliant plan. How did you come up with it? Did they accept the offer?"

"Wouldn't you? Mr. Smith, as he wants to be called, was thrilled to be paid double 'handsomely' to do the right thing without any risk of being caught or punished for doing the wrong thing."

"When will the second letter be ready?"

Before the Colonel can answer, Annabelle comes down the stairs and calls out. "Master Grant? Your bride iz ready. She's a-waitin' til the Reverend iz here 'fore you sees her, but she is so very gorgeous! Does ya needs anythin' from me, sir? I wants to wake lil' Mattie so she can be the flower girl. Would that be to your satisfaction, sir?" Annabelle does not wait for an answer. She curtsies and is off to wake her little girl.

Grant looks at the Colonel. "I should be nervous about getting married, but I am too excited. Do you know what it is like to wait for years to marry your love?"

"Actually yes. I do." Will says very quietly.

41

"Of course, you would know better than anyone. I am not thinking clearly. Now, when will that letter be done?"

The front door suddenly opens. Clarence calls out, "Master? Reverend Scott is here."

Grant jumps up from his seat, and rushes to the front door. "Reverend, so good of you to come out so late with so little notice." The Reverend and Clarence also shake off the snow. After thoroughly shaking the frozen man's hand, he says, "You are chilled to the bone, Reverend. Clarence, please go put on a pot of . . .what do you prefer, tea or coffee or hot chocolate?"

"Oh, hot chocolate sounds divine." The Reverend is a portly man with gray at his temples. When he smiles multiple dimples ripple through his cheeks.

"Clarence, make it so, please. Reverend, come into the front parlor and have a seat. My bride is ready, and as soon as you have warmed up by the fire, we can begin." He leans in closely to whisper. "I have an envelope here that, hopefully, will make up for the short notice and the dreadful weather." He turns to his brothers-in-law, "Gentlemen, meet Reverend Scott. Reverend these are my bride's brothers, Colonel William Clyde Lewis and Charles Palmer Lewis, but we call him Chilly." They all shake each other's hands.

The Reverend speaks first, "So very nice to make your acquaintances." He turns to Grant, "Young man, didn't you tell me some weeks back that you were going to Lawrence for your nuptials? Why are we doing them here and now?" As soon as he asks, he turns to the fire with his hands out to feel the warmth.

"Well, Reverend, a personal emergency has come upon us. I did not think it could be resolved in time to get to Lawrence. My bride-to-be, with her two brothers, came to help. That issued is still unresolved. I cannot explain it but with the plans still up in the air for me to leave, we thought that . . . I feel that . . . let me just be blunt. I cannot wait any longer, sir. I have waited for Carolyn for years. She agrees that we cannot – NO – will not wait another day to be husband and wife. Please Reverend, will you perform the ceremony for us? Carolyn and I will be devastated if you refuse."

The Reverend puts his hand on Grants shoulder. "Calm

yourself, young man. I have watched your affection for each other blossom over the years. She has attended services with you and your mother, many times. I will not break the lady's heart by refusing."

Grant grabs the Reverend's hand from his shoulder, and gives it another thorough pumping. "It would have broken my heart, as well, sir. Thank you SO much!" He turns to the Chilly. "Can you run upstairs, and tell the bride that we can proceed." He looks to the Reverend, "Are you sufficiently warmed up, Reverend?"

"I am after that last handshake. We can begin." Clarence has come in with a tray, filled with a large pot and several cups. He lays the tray down on the coffee table.

Annabelle comes out of the kitchen area with Matilda. Her dark little daughter is dressed up in a beautiful Sunday dress. Annabelle is a wonderful seamstress. She makes lots of dresses for herself, and her little girl. 'Fit for any white girl, they iz!' Clarence often says, proudly. Annabelle is dressed in her new Sunday dress that she just finished for herself. She is a very large woman, and the effort of quickly dressing the bride, Matilda, and herself is showing in the beads of sweat that she is dabbing with a white handkerchief.

Chilly is escorting his sister down the stairs. He calls to his brother. "Colonel, you get to walk her down the aisle, I am, apparently, the best man. So, let's switch places." Carolyn waits on the landing of the staircase for Will.

The Colonel stops at the parlor's threshold to look at the bride. "Obviously, Grant is trying to give me a run for 'The luckiest man alive' title. You are beyond stunning, sis. Are you ready?"

"I have never been more ready, brother. I just wish Mother and Father were here, but I am sure they will understand. Don't you?"

"They only want to see you happy. If they could see the smile on your face, right now, they would be very understanding." He holds out his arm for her, she takes it, and he says, "I am honored to bring you to your husband."

As Will and Carolyn enter the room, Annabelle begins to cry. Clarence has his arm around her, and is hugging her. "There, there, Annie." He says to try to quiet her. Matilda is all

**43**

smiles, but hides shyly behind her mother's skirt.

Carolyn is trying to concentrate on her steps, as she walks to her groom. Not until she is at his side, does she look up at him. He has tears in his eyes. "Grant, you always said that you don't like when women cry."

"I never understood how woman could feel things deep enough to bring them to tears. I love you so much, my heart is about to explode, and you love me too! How can I not cry?"

The Reverend clears his throat. "Shall we begin?" They all nod. "Dearly Beloved, we are gathered here today . . . I mean, tonight . . ."

The ceremony only takes a few moments, but Carolyn feels that it is in slow motion. She is holding her breath for the moment when the Reverend will say, 'You may kiss the bride.'

When he says it, she lets out her breath and leans in for their first married kiss. She says, "Oh, how I have waited for this kiss, my love."

His answer is his soft warm lips on hers. It is a long loving first embrace. He has never dared to kiss her like this before. He did not trust himself to be able to stop with just a kiss. He knew he would want everything from her. He reaches for her face, and holds it in place.

Finally, when the Reverend clears his throat again, they separate. The Reverend says, "I think a hot chocolate toast is in order! Congratulations, Mr. and Mrs. Grant Johnson.

Annabelle starts pouring. Grant notices that there are not enough cups for everyone. He looks to Clarence. "We are three cups, short. Please I want you, Annie and Mattie to join in the toast."

Annabelle smiles, "So kind, Master, but . . ."

"No arguing with me, Annie, you are family. Do you agree, my Wife?"

"Of course, my Husband. Go, Clarence, hurry before the chocolate cools." She turns to the Reverend. "We cannot thank you enough, for coming out at this hour. Did you want to wait until daylight before you travel back home? We can put you up for a good night sleep, and it will be warmer with the light of the day for traveling.

"That is so kind of you, Mrs. Johnson, but I think I need to be in my own bed tonight. If Clarence would be so kind to

**44**

take me back home. I wasn't thinking. I should have brought my own buggy for the trip back."

Grant says, "Nonsense, it is the least we can do for you. We are so very happy to be man and wife!"

After the toasts are made and the chocolate consumed, Clarence gets the buggy out to take the Reverend back home.

As Grant and Carolyn show the Reverend out, the Colonel and Chilly say good-night, and head up the stairs.

Alone at last, Grant looks at his beautiful wife. "My darling, let us have our own private toast."

She lifts the pot to refill the cups, "I am afraid we are empty, darling." As she looks up, Grant produces a bottle of champagne. "Were you expecting a celebration? Where did you get that?"

"I have my ways, my dear. I thought that a little drink would help us both with our nerves."

She goes to him, and reaches up for his face. "I love you so much, Grant. Kiss me."

He puts the bottle down, and takes her in his arms. "How I have dreamed of this." His lips are on hers, softly at first, then hungrily. Her passion rises to match his. His tongue seeks entrance, and she is taken aback by it. She, suddenly, breaks apart. "My dear?" He feels ashamed for already trying something for which she is not ready.

"I guess we do need that bottle, after all." She says meekly.

"Let me go in the kitchen for something to open it, and get two glasses."

"Yes, why don't I go upstairs to our room, and wait for you." As she says this, she blushes. "Do hurry, my love."

"Yes, ma-am. Your wish is my command." He starts off then suddenly stops and looks to her. "Darling, let me just say, as happy as I am to be your husband, I will still honor my pledge. I will only go as far as I am invited. Let that give you some piece of mind."

"I wasn't worried, my dear." She rushes to him, buries her head on his shoulder and whispers. "I love you so much, I want to give you, everything that I have to offer to prove it."

He picks up her head from his shoulder. "I feel the same way. I want to give you everything in my power to give you, to

**45**

prove how much I love you."

"You gave me your last name, and now a bottle of champagne. You are off to a very good start, for the first half-hour. Meet you upstairs, my love."

He turns to go, and thinks to himself, *I am the luckiest man alive!"*

# TEN

## Saturday, December 10<sup>th</sup>, 1882 in EL Dorado

The newlyweds did not leave their bedchamber until early afternoon. Annabelle brought up a tray for breakfast, announced its presence, and immediately went back down the stairs. She brought up a lunch tray the same way, and exchanged it for the empty breakfast one. The Colonel and Chilly went into town early, and spent the day. They sent a telegram announcing the wedding to both Mothers. They also did a little Christmas shopping.

They came home to find the couple in the parlor having late afternoon tea. Grant calls out to them to ask if they could join them.

"Will, I never got an answer last night, regarding the second letter. How soon will it be ready? And how much is 'double-handsomely'?

Will clears his throat. "I am glad you asked. I had to give him a deposit, and the rest is due at the time of completion. Mr. Smith expects it to be ready by Monday. It is going to cost you one thousand dollars."

Carolyn nearly spits out her tea. "Darling, do we have that much cash available?"

"Not in the house. I will need to go to the bank. I am surprised that my Uncle would have spent five hundred dollars on a scheme, such as this. That is a large sum, but if it keeps the estate in my name, it is money well spent. We, also, did not discuss when to take that road trip. I think we should wait until we have the letter in hand, so on Tuesday, we should head out." He looks at Carolyn. "Darling, can you be ready to take tonight's stagecoach to Wichita for a private honeymoon?"

"I can be ready in a half hour, but are you sure that we should spend the money with the large sum needed for the letter?"

"You are adorable, my dear. We can easily do both, I assure you. I will need to go to the bank before we depart. Colonel? Will you come with us to bring home the 'double-handsome' amount? The stagecoach leaves at 5 p.m.

**47**

promptly."

Carolyn puts down her tea cup. "Then we must leave right way. Grant? What will we do in Wichita?"

Instead of saying it out loud, he just leans over, and whispers in her ear. Carolyn blushes, then picks up her tea cup to drink it, but nervously swallows wrong, and starts coughing. Grant leans in again, and pats her on the back. "Was it something I said?" He asks.

All she could do is nod; then her coughing turns into nervous laughter.

Chilly looks at her, and says with all seriousness, "Let us in on the joke." That makes the Colonel and Grant explode with laughter, also. "Now, what is so funny?" For as tall as he is, Chilly still has a lot of growing up to do.

***

The stagecoach is late, but Mr. and Mrs. Grant Johnson are waiting comfortably in the EL Dorado Hotel for its arrival. They will spend the evening traveling, and will arrive around midnight. Carolyn is very excited. She has never seen Wichita. She is disappointed that she and her new husband need to spend the evening with other people present. She cannot wait to lie in her husband's arms, again. This time it will be in the exciting big town of Wichita.

# ELEVEN

## Sunday, December 11ᵗʰ, 1882 in Wichita

The stagecoach pulls up in front of the Wichita Arms Hotel at nearly one a.m. Grant has wired a reservation for a two-night stay. They will leave Monday afternoon. As he helps Carolyn out of the coach, he leans in to say, "Shall we have a light midnight snack? I am starving. A man needs to keep his strength up." He gives her a wink.

"I am starving, also, but can we check in, and go to our room first to . . . um . . . freshen up?" She winks back.

"I knew we would be a perfect match for each other." He looks at his watch. "Have I told you, this morning, that I love you?"

"No, my husband, it has been at least twelve hours since I have heard those words from you. That is very unsatisfactory!"

"I beg your pardon, Mrs. Johnson." He leans in even closer and kisses her cheek, while he whispers, "I love you." At this point, they are at the desk to register. "Good morning, my good man. We have a reservation under the name of Grant Johnson. For the Bridal Suite, if available?" Carolyn gasps at the thoughtfulness of her new husband,

They are escorted to their Suite. The bellboy has their bags, and sets them down. "Is there anything you need, sir or ma-am before I leave?"

Carolyn is amazed at the rich appointments of the suite. "Oh Grant, this is gorgeous! Can we get room service? I do not want to leave these rooms until we have to get back on that stagecoach!"

"As always, my darling, your wish is my command. Tell the man what you want. I have a taste for champagne with breakfast. I will have two eggs, a large steak, if you have one, with toast and coffee."

"I will have the same. Also, bring up some apple, no make that grape juice, if you have it. Bring up the beverages as soon as possible, please."

"Yes, ma-am, as you wish." The bell boy says as Grant

**49**

has his hand in his coin purse. He hands him a few coins. "Thank you, sir, you are most kind."

Carolyn is taking off her new hat and coat. As soon as the door closes she drops her articles. She runs to Grant and puts her arms around his neck. "I am the luckiest woman alive. I am going make you the perfect wife, my dear." She looks in his brown eyes. "Have I told you, this morning, that I love you?"

"I don't believe that you have! Remind me to hold that against you." His arms wrap around her waist, and he hugs her tight.

"Well, my husband, I love you, so very much." She kisses him slowly, lightly, but with a sweet passion, that is becoming wonderfully familiar, and they feel the world around them disappear as they become entranced by their own embrace.

They are still locked in each other's arms minutes later, when room service knocks on the door of their suite. He has a cart with all the beverages that they ordered.

# TWELVE

## Tuesday, December 12th, 1882 in EL Dorado

The newlyweds arrived back at the Farmhouse very late last night. Everyone already turned in for the night. On the foyer table were multiple telegrams for them with congratulations and best wishes. Carolyn was so happy that her brothers thought to telegram home. Her mother's telegram was lovely, no regrets that she missed the ceremony, but looking forward to the one yet to come.

Everyone is at the breakfast table at eight a.m. Chilly and Will had done a little more investigating while the couple was away. The Colonel has a plan for this afternoon's road trip.

Carolyn, again, expresses her concern. "I am worried. My three favorite fellas are up to something, and the fact that you are not including me is worrisome."

Will says to her. "I will take good care of your new husband, sis. If all goes well, we can leave for Lawrence by Thursday."

"Grant, I am exhausted from all the um . . . travel. Aren't you too tired to go for a horse ride?"

"I am fine, Carolyn. I am anxious to put an end to this nonsense." He turns to his brother-in-law. "Will, have you been in contact with Mr. Smith?"

"Yes, Saturday, I sent word to him that the funds would not be ready until this morning. He agreed to meet with us at eleven.

\*\*\*

The morning's meeting with 'Mr. Smith' went better than even the Colonel or Grant expected. The document looked as old as the one that Grant tried to rip up. The handwriting looked just as aged, and eerily similar to his mother's handwriting. 'Mr. Smith' admitted to more than expected. He dated it before Grant was born.

It read:

To Whom It May Concern – Dear Sirs,

**51**

I have had the privilege to create a document for Mr. Benjamin Johnson for which I was paid handsomely. In it, I was told to cast aspersions on the good name of Mrs. Mary Johnson and her son Grant – the true son of Steven Johnson, and heir to the Johnson Family Farms.

In order, to perfect the handwriting for the closest inspection, Ben Johnson gave me a group of letters from Mary Johnson to his Mrs., her step-sister-in-law. I take great pride in that letter. I imitated her speech pattern as well as her lettering. I aged it as I have aged this letter; which if I were a betting man, would hold up as authentically old in any court of law.

Mary's lovely letters to Mrs. June Johnson were full of stories of her romance with her husband. The letters after his death were full of sadness, but strength, too. She talked of moving to Lawrence for the sake of her children. She did not want to leave the home in which she had so many memories of her dear departed husband, but she said that she had to be strong for the only thing she had left of Steven – his children.

Having read this, I felt a tremendous sense of guilt, knowing that my masterpiece will bring down an innocent woman, and besmirch her good name. I was very happy when I was approached by an emissary of Grant's to find the man who forged the letter, so I agreed to a meeting. I was offered double the amount to admit to my part in the fraudulent letter. I agreed to accept the funds, but truth be told, I would have written this letter free of charge.

So here I sit, admitting to a terrible deed with a stack of large bills at my side. I hope that this letter does go to court, so that the man behind it all will be stopped, and shamed for trying to hurt a true patriotic strong woman, one - Mrs. Mary Johnson, who loved her husband very much –

.

Yours truly,
Mister John Smith

Professional Artist

Grant had to laugh at Mr. Smith's sense of honor for a forger. "Worth every penny!" Grant exclaimed, and shook the man's hand.

Later in the afternoon, the brothers-in-law are nearing a small cabin in the woods. Even from this distance they can tell that the roof has a hole in it, but smoke is coming out of the chimney. They leave their horses a distance down, and walk through the woods parallel to the road. As they get closer, they hear young children laughing. Grant leans in to Will. "I don't want anyone hurt, here. I am just looking for answers."

"That is all we want, also. Relax, Grant. Just because I was given the title of Colonel, it doesn't mean that I have ever been cruel."

"I didn't mean to imply that, Will. I am just nervous and talking. I have never done anything like this. I do not know what to expect."

"You stay hidden while I will knock on the door, and ask for Molly. Chilly can watch the back of the property. I will ask her a few questions, and you can intervene at any time. No one is going to get hurt by questions."

"Sounds easy enough. Let's go!"

With everyone in place, the Colonel goes onto the front porch. He quietly knocks on the door. It is quickly opened by a young light-skinned black girl of about ten. "I am looking for Molly. Is she home?" The little girl looks over her shoulder. She is soon joined by an older woman. "Are you Molly, then?" the Colonel asks.

The thirty-something light-skinned black woman shakes her head no, and turns her head, as the little girl did before her. She calls out "Molly!!" A girl a few years older than himself comes to the door. She looks up at the Colonel, then looks down to her feet.

"Are you Molly?" She nods her head. "Mr. Johnson sent me here." Will smiles for that is the truth.

Molly looks up. She has striking features that captures your attention immediately. She has deep, dark, soulful eyes surrounded by the longest lashes. She has her hair braided in rows that extend to her shoulder with a kerchief covering just

**53**

her crown. She steps outside the door and closes it. "Is he not visiting today?" She looks past the Colonel to peer down the lonely dirt road. "He told me he would come today. I have a meal at the ready."

"Oh, he will be here but a little late. I came to ask you a question or two, regarding the child. Can I see him?"

She goes back to the door, opens it and calls in the house. "Theo, come to mother." A moment later, a little light-skinned boy that resembles the girl more than the mother was standing before him.

"What did you want to ask about my Theo?" Molly has her arm around him. The little boy looks up, and the Colonel sees he has light hazel eyes. The little girl had them, also.

"What is that little girl to you?" He asks bluntly.

"She is Theo's half-sister. She is Sara's girl."

Grant cannot stand idle any longer. He jumps onto the porch from his hiding place. "Molly, who is their father?" She recognizes him, and backs up to the wall of the building. "Who?" He repeats.

Will leans over to Grant. "Look at Theo's eyes. They are hazel. What color are Ben's eyes?"

"His are brown, but Grandmother Antonia had light hazel eyes. My mother said that they were the only beautiful characteristic she had. Molly, you named your son after his grandfather – MY GRANDFATHER, Theodore Johnson? HE must be turning over in his grave!!" Grant starts to laugh at the thought, then gets serious. "Molly, do you know that Ben is threatening me with his - this child? Do you know what kind a man he is?"

"I love him. So, does Sara. He is good to us."

"So, he comes here to bed you both?"

Molly's blush gives him his answer. *So, Annabelle's rumors are all true,* he thinks.

"Why are you making trouble for me, Molly? I have never done anything to you. I was kind to you. Why would you be a part of this?"

"Ben said that I will not have to testify or anything. He said that I will always have a roof over our heads if I . . . help. I am sorry for it, Master Grant. I had to take care of myself and my child."

---

**54**

The Colonel steps forward suddenly. "What if I take you to Lawrence to live, and promise you a home and a job there?"

"Sir? Lawrence? That is far away, isn't it?"

"Far enough to keep you safe. Is it just Sara, the girl and yourself with Theo?" The Colonel asks.

"Yes, sir." She is looking at her feet again.

"I will give you all shelter, work on my lands, and you will have a better roof over your head than this. And no one will expect you to share your bed as a kept woman. Can you leave at once?"

She looks to Grant. "Sir, that's a very generous offer but I love Ben. I do."

Grant fires back. "He is using you! He cannot – *he will not* marry you or Sara, but he wants you to *lie* with him, *lie* for him, and then blackmail me! He is a dishonorable man, and has led you into a dishonorable life. We are offering you a clean slate with no judgement or repercussions. Do you understand?"

He pauses to try to read her blank face. He steps closer to lean in. "Or, I could have the law out here, have your little ones removed, and you tossed into jail for attempted blackmail. We are trying to help you . . . help all of you. I do not want to threaten you. Let us just help you. What time is Ben expected?"

"He always comes after sunset. I am not sure. I do know if he sees me, he will know that you have been here. He will know." She repeats, then puts her hands over her eyes. "He cannot see me. I am being forced to go, now. He will know that I was offered a better life. You must stop him from coming here or he will kill me when he sees me!"

"The man you love will kill you? How can you say you love him if you know he is capable of that?"

"You are right! Just help us, please? You have to help us!"

"We will get you packed up, quickly, and on the road. Do you have a horse or buggy?"

She shakes her head no.

"Okay, how much time is there?" He looks at his pocket watch as he says. "We need to do this NOW!" He looks back to Molly. "Let's get you and Sara on the road. Take only things that are sentimental.  We will replace everything else."

\*\*\*

Grant is soon in the lead on his horse Romeo.  The two other horses have a woman with her child on their backs with one of his brothers-in-law holding the reins.  They are making their way through the woods that is parallel to the road.

The weather has turned ugly.  The temperature has dropped and another snow storm is brewing.  No one has talked since leaving the broken-down cabin.

Grant is wondering how his new bride is going to accept the newcomers.  Even though she said she believed in his innocence, bringing the alleged 'other woman' to their home might be a step too far for their fledgling marriage.

As soon as they pass the crossroad that Ben would be taking, they all breath normally, again.  Grant stops, and turns his horse around.  "We need to make some time, now.  Will?  Chilly?  You need to get on your horse, behind the ladies now.  Can you ride like that?"  As an answer, both men swing up on their horses.  Grant gives a swift kick to Romeo, and they head to the Farmhouse with all haste.

With the horses riding at full speed, they arrive at the estate under two hours even with the snow now falling heavily.  As they pull directly into the stables, Clarence runs out to meet them.  As the women and children dismount, Molly turns to him.  "Clarence, it is good to see you again."  She puts her hand on her son's head.  "This is my boy Theo.  Theo, say hello to Clarence."

"You named the boy after that man?  That awful, awful, mean man?  What were you thinkin'?"  He says in disbelief.  "Molly, why?"

"His father named him after his father."  Molly says simply.

"That testimony that will put an end to any doubt!"  Grant says as he is leading Romeo to his stall.

"Thank God!  I was so worried that I was to be a widow before my big wedding!"  Carolyn shouts out as she is holding the stable door open with one hand, and has her cloak in her other.  Her red hair is down and blowing in the wind as the snow flurries around her.  "Grant, you took too long.  I was worried, so worried!"

Grant pats Romeo's nose as he turns to his wife. "There was no danger at all. My love, I was with the Colonel and Chilly. What could become of us? Why are you holding your coat instead of wearing it? Do you want the sniffles for your big wedding?" He goes to her, takes the coat from her hands, puts it around her shoulders and leans in. "You missed me, my wife? I will not tire of those words. *My wife.*" He kisses her on her lips softly, then turns to the others. "Carolyn, dear wife, come meet Molly. Meet my cousin Theo, too. The Colonel offered them homes and jobs in Lawrence."

Carolyn looks at the women, who were both born as slaves. One of whom almost cost her a husband, and she smiles at her and says, "I am so glad you are here. We will take care of you and your family." She looks to the other woman and the girl. "You are all welcome. Come, it is way too cold, now that the sun is down and snow is still falling. You must be frozen to death. We must get some hot food in all of you."

She leads the refugees into the kitchen entrance. "Annie, Mattie! We need food, and lots of hot beverages. Please hurry!"

# THIRTEEN

## Wednesday, December 13th, 1882 in EL Dorado

The Colonel is the first one up in the Johnson household. After supper, he had helped the women and their children get settled in Mattie's room for the night. It was agreed that everyone will leave for Lawrence this afternoon to take the odd family unit to his home. He has decided that both women can be inside servants since they both demonstrated last night, that they can cook very well. His mother has needed a house servant for some time now, but has refused. With Carolyn now married, she will need additional help. As Grandmother Marilyn gets on in years, she helps less and less. It is time, he gave back to these dedicated women, that have shaped his life.

Annabelle hears someone in *her* kitchen, and goes to see the Colonel putting a pot of coffee on for everyone, and putting on a kettle for tea for himself. He smiles at the memory of promising himself that he will no longer drink coffee after a private spilled a cup on one of the first letters from his Julia. He docked the Private a whole day's pay, and has preferred tea ever since.

"Colonel, why didn't ya'll call ole Annie to get this for you? I will have breakfast for you, right away, sir."

"Annie, I am very capable of making coffee and tea. I can even make eggs, if pushed." He gives her a large smile. "No one else would eat them though!"

Annie gives him a hearty laugh which made her belly shake. "Sir, you iz always good for a laugh. It is very nice of you to help young Molly. You and Master Grant have very big hearts. If it wuz up to me, I would not have helped her if she gimme half the trouble she tried to give Master."

"It's a good thing that it is not up to you, then." He walks over to Annabelle and gives her a hug. "And I think you are a bad liar, also. I will go wait in the dining room for my tea and eggs. I will take some meat on the side, if you have any on hand." He walks into the dining room.

Will is not alone for long. His sister comes down before

her husband, and looks around the dining room for something. "Isn't there coffee? I am nothing without my coffee." She smiles at her older brother.

"I made it myself, and I expect it out here at any time. Annie kicked me out of the kitchen." He gets up, and kisses his sister on the forehead. "And she hasn't even tasted my coffee yet."

"Well, let me go get it then. I really need it." She leaves for the kitchen while her husband Grant enters the dining room from the hall.

"Good morning, Will. Did you sleep, well?" He sits down at the table. His wife comes back in with a tray of coffee and cups. "Look at my bride, she is just amazing, isn't she?" He gets up, goes to his wife, and takes the tray from her. "Did you see how she brought Molly and Sara into the house like they were Queens, and not ex-slaves trying to blackmail me. She has a big heart, just like you, Colonel. She already acts like the Mistress of my home, as if she has been doing it her whole life. I have never been so in love."

Carolyn has been busy pouring the coffee into the cups. "Grant, you are making me blush. Stop that!"

"I love to make you blush. I like watching to see if the blush is going to outdo that flaming red hair!" He looks at Will. "I almost did it when I told her what we were going to do in Wichita. I came this close!" He holds out his fingers showing a half inch space between his index finger and thumb.

Carolyn hands him his coffee, and once her hands are free, she swats him on the chest. "Be nice, Grant! At least until we have breakfast. We have a big day ahead of us. What time are we leaving for Lawrence?"

"I'd like to be on the road by two, if we can."

\*\*\*

It is three in the afternoon when they are finally packed up for their journey. They are taking two buckboards to Lawrence. Grant wants to get out of EL Dorado with Molly and Sara as quickly as possible. He did not want his Uncle to be able to stop him. The 'double-handsome' letter is in his safe deposit box at the bank waiting for the time his lawyers are contacted by his Uncle's lawyer, if ever. Annie has gone out of her way to provide sandwiches, cheese wheels and breads for the journey.

The only problem with the timing of traveling right now is that Joan of Arc still has not begun her foaling process. Clarence insists he will send a telegram when she gives birth. He hasn't told Carolyn, yet. He still wants to surprise her with the foal.

The little girl Antonia and Theo bicker throughout the first hours of the ride. Grant cannot believe that his uncle named both of his bastard children after Ben's parents. Several times, the mothers try to intervene, but distraction is what is needed. Carolyn climbs into the back with the children, and sings a new Christmas song with them. The mothers love the song, and Carolyn teaches it to all of them. Both children are thrilled with the personal attention.

They stop in the town of Florence for a late supper. They have already secured three rooms for the night.

Walking back from supper, Antonia asks, "Do we still have a long ride, Mistress?"

"Yes, it will take a few days riding. You will like Lawrence. It has been my home my whole life."

"Are there other children my color there?"

This makes Carolyn think a minute. "There is a section of town where negroes live, but I have never been there. You will be living with my family, and your mother will be their house servant. There is a much to do on our farm. There will never be a lack of work for you or Theo or your mother. You must attend school, though."

"School? What is that?" Antonia looks up at her with her hazel eyes wide open with curiosity. "Is that like church? I have to attend that."

Carolyn puts her arm around her small shoulders. "Well, church teaches you about God. School teaches you about reading and counting. You will make lots of friends there."

"That sounds very nice, Mistress."

"I loved school. I didn't do very well in it but I had many friends. I did better once my sister-in-law started helping us with our homework. She always made it fun. Mrs. Julia is the

Colonel's wife and a delight. The Colonel will have Molly as his house servant. He promised you a roof over your head better than the leaky one you had. The Colonel is very good at keeping his promises."

She smiles at Will as he turns to bend low to say in a mock whisper to the little girl. "I don't make promises that are hard to keep. That's my secret."

Carolyn laughs. "Such chivalry! My brother is a true knight from the tales of Arthur and Camelot!" She looks down at Antonia. "A great tale to read when you learn how. That was the best thing about school - learning to read. All the wonderful Worlds written about in the pages of books are waiting for you. So many exciting people and stories! I love to read. I can hardly stand it when a book ends. Then I start another, and am lost again."

"Oh, I cannot wait until I can read!" Antonia smiles widely.

"One of the great things about Grant's Farmhouse is its library. They have a thousand books that are waiting to be cracked open, and the world within discovered."

"You are making me want to read, sis."

"It couldn't do you any harm. Julia has a nice collection of books. The best homes have a decent private library, I think."

Grant is walking a step behind his wife. "Carolyn, you have been enjoying our books for years. By the way you are putting it, you married me for the house's library."

"Well, the library was the cherry on top of the sundae, my husband. I intend to have either you or a book in my arms all the times. You don't mind, do you?"

"Not if I come first and foremost."

"Always, my love." She stops walking, and turns to him to put her arms around him. "First and foremost, I promise." She leans in and lightly brushes her lips over his, then whispers. "Let's not spend too long saying good-night, my love. I have plans for you." Then she blushes.

He looks at her. "There is that blush that I love! Even in this night lighting, it is competing with your hair for the title 'Most Red'. Never stop blushing, my girl."

"I will do my best, my love." She drops her arms, but

**61**

takes his hand. "Look how far they are ahead of us. Let's catch up, shall we?"

The newlyweds run all the way to the hotel, where they bid everyone a good night, and disappear into their room.

# FOURTEEN

## Thursday, December 14, 1882 in Kansas

The travelers are up early, and have breakfast in the Florence Hotel restaurant. Afterward, Will and Chilly go to the Livery to get the buckboards. Carolyn goes into the General Store that is across the street. She is looking for a specific item. Grant, Molly, Sara, and the little ones wait out in front of the hotel for the buckboards.

Carolyn comes out of the store at the same time Will and Chilly pull up to the hotel. She has a wrapped package in her hands, and looks up and down the street. She runs to the waiting group. Grant helps her up into the front seat of the buckboard while Chilly helps load the women and children into the back.

Grant gets in himself, and looks to his new bride. "What is in the package? A memento from our marriage travels?"

"No, since I was telling Antonia about books, I thought I would buy one to read to her on the trip. Nothing like inspiring a young mind. Don't you think?" The group heads off toward their next stop. They get an hour away when they hear hooves behind them. The road that they are traveling has thick woods on either side, so the sound is magnified. The Colonel looks back toward Grant, who is looking behind also. Grant stops looking at the horses behind him, and looks up at Will with panic on his face. He tries to yell to him, but the Colonel cannot make out the words. The Colonel grabs his rifle next to him, and gives Chilly the reins. "Don't stop, boy. There is trouble brewing behind us. I am going to try to tell Grant to pass us so I have a good shot."

He has his rifle with him as he climbs over the seat onto the buckboard. He is motioning to Grant to come forward. Grant seems to understand, and gives a yell to the horses followed by a crack of the whip. As he comes even with the Colonel, he yells. "That is Ben's henchman Thornton, a hired gun." That is all he has time to say as the rig moves past the Colonel.

Grant hands the reins to Carolyn. He grabs his rifle,

and looks to the women and children. "Get down, now. Lay down flat as you can." They all lay down. He turns back to his wife. "Can you get in the buckboard and lay down? I never thought he would follow us, but I will have you safe."

Carolyn looks at him. "Give *me* the gun. I am a much better shot. You take the reins." Grant hesitates. "You know that I can outshoot you, Darling. Don't be vain at a time like this!" Reluctantly, he exchanges the gun for the reins, and she maneuvers effortlessly over the seat, even in her long skirt. She makes her way past the prone family, and lies on her own stomach with the rifle firmly in her hands aimed out of the carriage at the intruders.

The Colonel sees that Thornton and his three men are coming closer. They are almost to the back of the buckboard. "Stop right there!" He shouts out to them.

"This is a public road, mister. I am trying to get to Emporia by nightfall."

"Thornton, I said stop where you are." As the man starts to pass him the Colonel lets off a warning shot. "Do you want a bullet in your back, Thornton?"

Thornton and his men slow down. "How do you know my name, Mister?"

"I know that you work for Benjamin Johnson. Now go back to him and tell him to leave us alone, or your men will bury you here in the countryside." The Colonel raises the rifle and aims for Thornton's head.

As this is happening, two of the men pull back on their horse's reins and fall back behind, then maneuver the horses to come up on the other side of the buckboard. One of the men has his gun drawn. They are staying even with the backside of the buckboard.

Carolyn is watching closely through the sights of her rifle. She sees her big brother surrounded, so she fires a low warning shot at the man at Will's back. The shot hits the dirt just in front of the first horse's feet. This makes the horse buck and the armed man gets thrown off. She cocks the rifle, again, and aims for the other rider, who luckily did not trample the first man. That rider does not have a gun drawn, so she hesitates.

The Colonel yells to Chilly. "Whoa, Chilly. Let's slow

down to talk." Grant is looking over his shoulders, and doesn't know if he should continue the pace or slow down also. As if sensing it, the Colonel waves Grant to keep going.

Carolyn yells to her husband. "I can't protect him if we get too far away!"

"You can't get shot either. Let Will handle this."

Carolyn watches helplessly as Grant drives further and further from her brothers.

Chilly brought the buckboard to a stop. The Colonel is talking to Thornton and his men. Carolyn cannot make out what is going on. "Grant, please stop. What is happening back there? I cannot tell."

"The Colonel told me to go, Carolyn."

"I am telling you to STOP! I mean it Grant, stop this buckboard, NOW!"

Even though she had been yelling all her sentences, he can tell that she is now mad, and means what she is saying. "Carolyn, the Colonel can take care of himself. He . . ." Grant can see that Carolyn is standing in the buckboard. She is leaning over the side rails. *She looks like she is going to jump out!* "Carolyn, stop right there. Okay, I will slow down."

"No, stop!"

Grant pulls on the reins for the team to come to a halt. Everyone in the first buckboard has eyes searching through the dust cloud kicked up by the horses to see what is happening. Suddenly, there is a shot. Molly screams. She is no longer lying flat. "He is gonna get us and make us pay, he is!" She starts to wail, and carry on.

Carolyn looks over her shoulder at the woman who is at least ten years older than her. "Stop that, this instant. This is no time for hysterics. Do you hear me."

The dust is settling, but the buckboards are too far apart from each other to tell what is going on.

"We can't just sit here. Turn around. Thornton won't expect us to come at him." Carolyn suggests.

"Only if you come up here. I don't need you trying to jump out on me. We have a big wedding to attend." She works her way to the front again.

She doesn't climb over the seat, but stands behind it. "Turn us around, my husband. We won't have a wedding to attend if something happens to one of my brothers."

As they are arguing about it. Antonia yells, "Mistress, they are a-comin'! Just the buckboard, not the bad men."

"Oh, thank God!" says Carolyn. They do not move an inch until Will's buckboard is next to theirs. "What happened?"

"I gave them a message to take to ole Uncle Benjamin. I told them that we know that he is the father of both children. Naming them after his parents wasn't the brightest thing to do. I told Thornton to tell Ben only to contact you through your attorney. They didn't see them in your buckboard." He nods to the women. "Thornton says that he thought they were in Emporia, with family that Sara has there. I told him that they were in Wichita, and that he was going the wrong way. I threw a twenty-dollar gold piece at him. He liked that move."

"But, there was another shot fired?" Carolyn says as a question.

"The horse you made buck broke his leg; so did his rider. Thornton shot the horse."

"So, he doesn't know that Molly is with us?"

"No." The Colonel chuckles. "The idiots didn't have a clue. They really were going to Emporia to look up Sara's relatives."

Sara now standing, speaks. "But Colonel, how did you know that I also have folks in Wichita?"

Every one laughs.

"Just a lucky guess, I guess. Now let's get moving. I want to make Emporia by tonight." The Colonel says as he climbs back onto the seat of the buckboard.

Chilly adds, "Yea, me too. A shoot-out can make a guy just about starve to death!"

The Colonel looks to his sister. "That's our growing boy, always starving!"

Molly offers "We still have cheese and bread from Annie." She goes into a basket, and hands Chilly a whole wheel of cheese. "There young man, start on this."

The rest of the ride to Emporia is uneventful. Will insists that Grant stay the lead buckboard. Carolyn once again sat in the back, and sang with the littles ones. The Colonel sat in the back of Chilly's buckboard facing the rear, scanning the horizon for trouble, which thankfully never came.

# FIFTEEN

## Friday, December 15th, 1882 Kansas

Grant is awake before the sun is up. He automatically reaches for his bride, but decides not to disturb her. She is snuggled around her pillow, facing him. Her waist length hair is in a loose braid, but some of it has escaped, and is framing her delicate face with red wisps. She is so beautiful, and HIS wife. He still cannot believe he is so lucky. He watches her sleep as the sun rises.

The first morning rays reach their pillows, and Carolyn can sense the daylight. She sighs before her eyes flutter open. This is the third day in a row that Grant has watched her wake, and it is always the same. She sees him watching her, and she is embarrassed by it. "Darling? Must you watch me every morning? I would hate for you to see me drool or something while still dozing." She gives him a small shove with both hands, but Grant catches her wrists before they get too far away. He has them in his hands as he rolls on top of her. He, now, has her arms above her head on the pillow.

"My dearest . . ." is all he takes time to say. His lips are on hers, and she is responding to them in a now familiar way. She loves this 'take charge' sort of passion, but thinks that it is her turn to control the situation. He has let go of her wrists, and one hand is under her gown feeling her curves.

She suddenly breaks apart from his embrace, and before he knows what is happening, she has him on his back with his wrists pinned down. This Carolyn is going beyond where she has felt comfortable, and is trying something new. She looks down at him. "Do you mind being a little adventurous?" As she says this, her hand is making its way down to his manhood.

"I am a most willing particip . . ." She doesn't let him finish his word or his sentence. Her mouth is on his, demanding his full attention. He closes his eyes, to enjoy what she has in store for him. She has never been so bold. "Oh, Carolyn. What do you have in mind?" Without saying a word, Carolyn adjusts herself, and she leads his part into her

**67**

warmness. "Oooohhh Carolyn," he utters.

After they are both drained and satisfied, Carolyn is cuddled up in his arms. "Was that too bold of me?"

Grant looks at his blushing bride. "You amaze me more every day I am with you. I never knew how much pleasure there was to being married. Did you know? I mean, did you think this was possible?"

"I thought so, my parents were very happy to be married. I suspected that they thoroughly enjoyed their marriage bed, by how many siblings I have. Which reminds me, how many children would you like to have?"

"I will take as many as God gives us. Or if he doesn't, I will be happy to have you all to myself for the rest of my days. Do you have a number in mind?"

"I would like a small family. Not a brood like the one I was raised in. I would like a boy for you, and a girl for me, but no more than three or four children, altogether." She starts to rise. "I think we need to get down to breakfast. Don't we have lots of miles to ride today? I hope to be in Lawrence before tomorrow night."

"Why? Do you have plans?" He says as he is rising.

"No, I just cannot wait to bed you in my room. I have been dreaming of you from that bed in my room for years. Now, you are all mine to have, and to hold from this day forward!"

"Won't you feel funny with your family in the next rooms? I think, I will. Maybe we ought to get a room at a hotel?"

"Nonsense, my husband. You will just have to get over your embarrassment. Like I did that first time I saw my brothers, after our wedding night. That was very awkward for me."

"You hid it very well. You seemed very casual about it all."

"It was the Colonel that I couldn't make eye contact with. He had his own momentous wedding night, if you recall, so he would know exactly what we were doing all night."

"And all morning!"

"Yes, and all morning." She smiles at the memory. "It was a wonderful wedding night. You were a true gentleman to your inexperienced wife."

"My dear, what we lack in knowledge, we make up for in our love for each other. May I tell you a secret?"

"Yes, please." She is at the dressing table putting her hair up for the day. She stops to give him her full attention.

"I am just as inexperienced as you. I have never been with a woman, Carolyn. That is why I know that I did not have anything to do with Molly. I would think that I would remember my first time, if she was it. My mother told me when I was a boy that the physical act is nothing without being in love. I have never <u>wanted</u> to be with a woman, without loving her first. So, I waited to fall in love. And just my luck, I had to wait another three years, because you were not old enough to wed. It was a very long three years! I thought about you all the time."

"And I, you!" She stands up, and goes to him. He is putting on his suit coat already, and she puts her arms under his coat and her head on his shoulder. "I hope I was worth the wait. I am so very happy. I love you so much."

"And I, you!" He says simply. "Now let's get a move on, my dear. We have miles to put on, today if we want to be in Lawrence before nightfall tomorrow." He winks at her.

The Colonel and Chilly were already at a large table in the richly appointed hotel restaurant when Grant and Carolyn join him. Moments later the children and their mothers come in, and sit down. The restaurant owner comes over to the table, indignantly. "We don't serve their kind here. They must leave, now, please."

The Colonel stands up. "They are part of our group, SIR. I must insist that they be served."

Grant and Chilly are now on their feet, also. The owner looks at all the men towering over him. "You can all leave, or I will call for Sheriff Brown. I am not looking for trouble, but . . . I have the other diners to think about. *They* are not comfortable with *their kind* eating off the same plates that they do."

Now Carolyn stands. "Poppycock! I did not see anyone looking uncomfortable until you approached our table, sir." She looks over to Grant. "Remind me to put an ad in the town's newspaper about their unwelcoming attitude. I might put an ad in Lawrence and Florence's papers also. 'When in Emporia –

do not eat at the hotel's restaurant', it will say. I have a while to plan it, but with your permission, husband, I would like to run it for a few months." She looks at the owner. "How will that help your business?"

"That's blackmail!"

The Colonel responds, "Well, these are black females and their children. They are equal to us, sir, and should be treated as such. Let's leave, everyone; I would not trust the food here, anyway." He takes a bill out of his billfold and throws it down on the table. "This should cover our beverages."

As they are walking out, Antonia says, "But I am so hungry! What are we going to eat?"

Sara just grabs her daughter, and pulls her close. "Don't worry 'bout it none, chile, we'z in good hands. I can see these are a better class o' white people then we'z used to." Sara looks from the Colonel to all the others. "Thank you. I have never felt so . . . grateful. No one's ever fought for us, b'fore. 'Cept the war, o'course, but not up personal-like, fightin' right in front of us – FOR US! The other Mr. Johnson wouldn't have."

Grant looks to her and Molly. "I don't think he would have had you at his table to begin with. That was not how he was raised." They are in the hotel lobby. "Let's check out, and get on the road."

"What about food?" Chilly, Carolyn and Antonia say at the same time, with a loud stomach noise coming from Chilly for emphasis.

The Colonel speaks up. "I will run to the General Store for bread, cheese, sweet cakes, sandwiches, and anything else there is to eat. Chilly, go get our stuff out of the room, and get the buckboards. I will meet you all out front with some goods."

"Don't forget coffee!! I would have ordered some from room service had I known that it was going to be so long before my first cup!" complains Carolyn.

It takes everyone about fifteen minutes before they are back in the lobby with their bags. As they all walk out into the street together, a rider pulls up to the hotel and Molly gasps. This makes Sara turn, and she gives a yelp. Both women instinctively move behind the six-foot-eight redheaded Chilly. Chilly looks to the children. "Get behind your mothers, little ones."

Grant steps forward. "Ben, don't start anything. These ladies have made up their minds."

Ben slowly gets off his horse. As he is tying him to the post, another rider barrels in, and aligns his horse next to Ben's. Ben says, "I am not the one causing the problem, here. Molly, Sara, come on home."

Molly peeks from behind Chilly. "No, Ben, this is going to be so much better for Sara 'n me. We ain't gonna have a leaky roof, we are going to have good jobs, and even schoolin' for the children."

Thornton gets off his horse. "Where is the tall guy with the beard? He is the one who told me that you were on your way to Wichita."

"RIGHT BEHIND YOU!" This made both men turn to see the Colonel, rifle in hand, looking down at both Thornton and Ben. "I thought we were done with you, Thornton. Do we have a problem here?"

"I think kidnapping is a problem! Thornton, go find the sheriff." Thornton takes two steps when the Colonel cocks the rifle.

"You are the second person today to threaten us with the sheriff, and I have yet to have my breakfast. I am very cranky before breakfast. Go get the sheriff. The women have come with us of their own free will. So, whom did we kidnap?"

"Antonia and Theo are my children. You cannot take them away from me."

Grant has his arm around Carolyn. "Thank you for admitting that in front of my bride, *Uncle Ben*. Not that she ever believed otherwise. But we are running late. If you'd just step aside, and let us all get on our way."

Ben looks to his man. "Thornton, what are you waiting for? Go, get the Sheriff!"

Sara steps forward. "There'z no need. These children are ours, and you ain't got no say in where we live. We both want a better life. One that you never did give us."

Ben takes a step closer. "You uppity Nigger! Watch your mouth to me!" He raises his hand to slap her, but Chilly steps forward, and grabs his hand in mid-air.

With the air of a man much older, Chilly says, "That is

one of the things these ladies will not miss.  Do you slap them around often?"  He takes the arm, and twists it behind Ben's back.  "Time to go back to EL Dorado, Mr. Johnson.  Just you and Thornton."

Carolyn, who has been very quiet up to now, looks to Grant.  "Husband, please introduce me to your uncle before he leaves."

Grant looks at his bride, and smiles.  "So sorry, my dear.  Uncle Ben, please meet my beautiful new bride, the former Carolyn Lewis.  These are her brothers, Colonel William and Chilly Lewis.  Your plans did not stop my bright future from becoming a reality.  Carolyn is the new mistress of the Johnson Farmhouse.  We were wed there last week.  You tried to ruin my life, but Carolyn did not scare off.  Her brothers have found the man who forged the letter, so that plan is over, also.  I'd say, 'no hard feelings', but I think I am going to remember what you tried to do for a long time.  We do have to get going now, so please step aside, *Uncle*."  He steps forward, and takes Chilly's hand off Ben's arm.  "You will let us leave unmolested now, right, Ben?"

Molly speaks for the first time.  "It's over, Ben.  We are leaving.  Say good-bye to Antonia and Theo, now."  She takes her boy's hand, and walks up to Ben.  "Theo, say good-bye to your Paw-Paw."  Little Theo holds out his hand for Ben to shake it.  Ben just looks down at the boy who has his mother Antonia's eyes.  "Get him away from me.  Good riddance to all of you.  Grant, you will still pay for taking away my home."

"It wasn't me, *Uncle*, it was Grandfather's trust that took your home away.  He could have changed it, but he didn't.  I guess he didn't care if you had the home or not.  Give it up, Ben.  I would have loved it if you, your wife and children were real family to us.  You've made it next to impossible."

Will says, "Ben, are we done here?  Are WE going to have to get rough with you or get the sheriff?  I am good either way.  Just walk away, is my suggestion.  Better yet, get on that horse, and get back to EL Dorado."  Ben finally moves, and goes to his horse.  He doesn't say a word.  He looks at Thornton, who moves to his horse, also.  They untie the horses, mount up, and Ben kicks his horse hard to take off.  No one says a word until their dust settles.  "Chilly, let's get the buckboards.  I need to go back and pay for the food I just picked out. We have miles to make up for the time this little family reunion took up! Any objections, anyone?"

They all shake their head, no, in unison.

# SIXTEEN

## Saturday, December 16<sup>th</sup>, 1882 in Lawrence

The little town of Lyndon had only two rooms available in their small hotel. Chilly and Will slept in the livery in the buckboards. The livery, though drafty, was reasonably warm. It was better than sleeping outdoors, as they were forced to do on their trip to find their nephew, two years earlier. Carolyn started to object saying that all the girls sleep in one room, and the boys all sleep in another, so that everyone could have a fire while they slept. The Colonel insisted that she and Grant not separate this soon after their vows. Chilly was going to argue, but Will gave him a little kick to the shin which meant 'keep your mouth shut'.

The little restaurant in the hotel opened at five a.m., and both Chilly and Will were seated, drinking their morning hot drinks within minutes of the door's opening.

Grant and Carolyn came down at six a.m.. Carolyn says to Chilly and the Colonel, "Dear brothers, was it warm enough? Did you get any sleep?"

"We managed a few hours. We will be home tonight, so I will be in my Julia's arms, and I will forget all about the cold."

"Lucky for you. What will I have?" Chilly complains.

"Your sister's deep affection and appreciation, and our mother's love." Carolyn kisses her younger brother on his cheek. Luckily, he is sitting down, she would have to do it on her tiptoes, if he were standing.

After Carolyn and Grant are given coffee, Molly and Sara come into the room with the children. Molly looks around, and bends down to Carolyn. "Mistress, we will wait for you in the lobby. No need to start a ruckus like yesterday. If it's not too much trouble, save us some biscuits for the road."

"Poppycock! You will have more than that. Waiter, please." The young man hurries over. "Is there any reason why my servants cannot be served with us. We are anxious to get on the road."

The young man looks nervously about. "I haven't heard no reason not to, ma-am. Do you know what they want to

74

have?" He gets his pad out, and licks the tip of his pencil to start writing. Carolyn orders ham and eggs with coffee for the women, and oatmeal and milk for the young ones.

After he leaves, Carolyn looks over to them. "See, no ruckus at all. Such nonsense that was yesterday! I'd like to forget everything about yesterday morning, altogether!" She starts to hum the new Christmas song, and to her surprise, everyone at the table joins in.

After everyone is breakfasted and full, they check out of their rooms, and start on their last leg of the trip. The weather has taken a warming turn for a change, and Carolyn feels that she can finally read to Antonia and Theo while riding in the open buckboard.

The book that she bought was *The Legends of King Arthur and his Knights of his Round Table,* by Alfred Lord Tennyson. She sat in the back of the buckboard and within a few pages she had Antonia, Theo and the mothers all spell bound by the first deeds of Merlin the Magician. Hours of traveling sped past, as she read aloud of King Arthur, his sword Excalibur, all of the knights, and of course his queen, Guinevere.

They stop for a late lunch in Ottawa. The sun is shining brightly, and the children having sat so still in the buckboard captivated by Carolyn's reading, are running up and down the sidewalk before coming into the restaurant. Carolyn has, again, checked with the person seating them if the ladies and children will be allowed to join them. Her polite, but direct approach, once again pays off and they are allowed in.

Once everyone has ordered, Carolyn says, "Do not dawdle, everyone. I really want to get home posthaste!" The women and children just look blankly at her. "That means in a hurry!" She looks to her brother. "Should we send a telegram to announce our arrival?"

"Great idea, sis. I will get right on that as soon as I eat. I am very anxious to get back to my wife, also. I think we are going to give the horses a workout!"

\*\*\*

It is less then four hours later that the two buckboards ride onto the plantation land. Though the hour is late, and the

**75**

temperature still cold, the family is all out on the porch, when they drive up.

Chilly has the reins, and has barely pulls the team to a stop when his older brother jumps off the moving vehicle, and runs to his beloved.

Will takes Julia in his arms, looks her up and down, and shouts, "Still, the luckiest man alive!!" Then he bends down to put his lips to his waiting wife's. She puts her arms around his neck, and he picks her up, and swing her all around. "God, how I missed you, my darling! Are you well?" As he is asking her this, he is kissing her on the mouth and face. She is crying and laughing at the same time.

"Oh, my husband, you were gone too long on your mission. I have missed you, terribly. Did you save my brother, then?"

The rest of the group are out of the buckboard. Grant walks to his sister. "He and Chilly did save me, and were my best men at our wedding, sis. Thank you for allowing him to leave your side. I know what a big sacrifice that is for you."

Carolyn is surrounded by her parents, and her older sister Marjorie. They are hugging her, and kissing her. Finally, Marjorie says, "Let's go inside, and you can tell us all about the wedding."

Carolyn blushes, "It was a lovely simple ceremony. Just a rehearsal for the big wedding on the Eve of Christmas Eve. Mama, are you mad at me for getting wed without you?"

As they are entering the house, Elizabeth Lewis answers. "I was disappointed, at first. But I understand why you didn't wait. When love calls, we trip over ourselves to answer, don't we? The only question that I would ask is *Are you happy*?, but I can see by your glowing look that I have my answer. We are so very happy for you, my girl."

Once inside, they discover that Grandfather Clyde, Grandmother Marilyn and Mother Mary are waiting for them, as well. Grant rushes to his mother. "Mother, I am sorry that you weren't at the ceremony. That was the only dim spot in the quick, but wonderful event. Do you forgive us?"

"Considering that I thought you were deathly ill or some other dastardly evil befell you, I was most happily surprised at the telegram Will sent us. Congratulations, my son. Carolyn, daughter, please come give Mother a hug, also." The newlyweds both heartily embrace the demure dark haired woman. "Seriously, Grant, you gave us all a fright! What was it all about?"

Still outside, Chilly and his father have gotten all the bags out of the buckboards, and give the horses to Stapleton, the twenty-three-year old negro in charge of the stable. Chilly calls out to him. "Give them extra oats and a good brushing, please. We rode them all pretty hard today."

Stapleton isn't listening. The young negro women and children have his complete attention. They are still standing outside, not knowing where to go. Chilly looks to his father. "Have you made arrangements for our new help, Father?"

William looks to the women. "Ladies, Stapleton will take you to your new quarters. When the Colonel and Julia leave for their little house, Molly and the boy will be going with them. STAPLETON, do you hear me? Show the ladies to their quarters, and take care of the horses."

This gets Stapleton moving. He very quietly says, "Ladies . . ." and points to the direction of several small cabins, that are beyond the stable. "This way, please." He adds. The ladies grab their few belongings and follow Stapleton.

William and Chilly go into the house, and set the bags down. Everyone is sitting around the dining room table, and talking at once. Julia is sitting on Will's lap, with her arms around his neck. They are staring into each other's eyes. She leans in and whispers. "It is so good to have your arms around me again, my darling."

"I think you have lost some weight again, Julia. Have you been unwell?"

"Just worried, and missing you, terribly. I have had very little appetite."

Mother Beth hears this. "She has barely eaten since you left. I hope that she remedies that, now that you are back to her." With that she passes a plate of cakes to her daughter-in-law. "Start with these."

Chilly interrupts. "We need something more than cakes, Mother. We have not eaten for hours, and I am starving!"

Grandmother Marilyn gets up. "I should have bet that Chilly would be hungry. When hasn't he been, in the last fifteen years?" They all laugh as Marjorie, Beth and Marilyn go into the kitchen to make sandwiches from the left over roast beef that they had earlier.

# SEVENTEEN

## Sunday, December 17th, 1882 in Lawrence

Julia wakes at first light. She is in her favorite spot, the arms of her husband. *It is so good to have him back.* While she is watching him, he sighs and stirs. As his eyes open he smiles. "I knew you were watching me. You always do, don't you?"

She smiles back at him. "It is time to rise. I expect Molly will arrive shortly to start work. Do you trust her? After what she tried to do?"

"It wasn't her. It was the uncle behind it all. He had both ladies in one cabin to have at his will. Just deplorable! How could any man raised Christian reconcile such behavior?" He looks at his pocket watch on the small table next to him. "It is not yet seven. Lay back down for a little while, dear. I have missed you so much."

She willingly folds herself into his arms. "And I missed you, my dear. Mother Beth is so wonderful, but I missed being in our little house."

"Which reminds me, I was thinking of a new house plan. I heard that the Jessup land has been put on the market. It is the perfect time to buy, and build you a larger home."

"We haven't outgrown this one, yet."

"Well, yes, we have. I would like Molly and her son to have their own quarters. I could build an attachment to this house, but I think a whole new house is in order, as I promised in my letters."

"I remember the promise, but what was the reason behind it? I forget."

"I promised to keep building a bigger home, as a testament to my ever-growing love for you"

"Do you think that your father's love for your mother is any less for not having built her home after home?"

"Theirs was a different time. He struggled to feed the growing mouths to be building from scratch. Our status in the community has grown and we can afford a bigger and better home."

"Your mind is made up, then?"

"Yes, I have the whole house built in my mind's eye. It will have a second floor with three bedrooms, and an attached servant's quarters. I cannot wait to get started."

"Will, I know that once your mind is made up, there is no stopping you. You are too good to me, my darling." She kisses him tenderly. "Now, let me show you how much I appreciate and love you for it, before Molly comes to work."

He rolls on top of her. "What did you have in mind, my bride?"

\*\*\*

Carolyn awakens in her childhood bedroom, with Grant once again, watching her sleep in the dim light of sunrise. She smiles, "I told you to stop that. Hasn't it grown old yet?"

"I pray that it never does. I am still so happy that you are finally mine."

"I am thrilled to be so. I must get up. I need to go to Grandmother's for another fitting of my wedding dress before Church service. Our wedding is Saturday, and there isn't much time. We were in the middle of pinning when your telegram came, and I practically tore the thing off me after reading your message. I was so upset, I even threatened to cut off all my hair to make you pay for hurting me. I don't take bad news very well, it seems."

"I will make a note of that. Your beautiful hair, Carolyn? You do know how to cut me to the quick if you thought of that as a punishment. I have been dreaming of your hair falling down around me as you made love to me for years!"

She blushes past her hair color, once again. "Picturing that, I um, think that Grandmother will just have to wait for that fitting." She takes her hair out of its sleep braid, and runs her fingers through it. Then she rolls on top of him, and lets it fall over him. "Is this what you imagined?"

He barely could say, 'exactly' before her mouth was on his, and she slowly took everything he had to offer.

Afterward, Carolyn says, "Now, you've fulfilled my dream of having you in this very room! I really, must go to Grandmother's. She said that she will have coffee waiting for me. I do love Grandmother's coffee, she makes it with a bit of chicory, you know."

Grant rises. "I know. It is delicious. I do need to talk with Mother. I will come with you."

"You can't see the dress, Grant. Promise you will leave before the fitting. Or we will have bad luck! A groom should never see the bride in her dress before the wedding!"

"I have no intention of causing us bad luck, but I do need to tell Mother of *her* letter. We did not bring it up last night in front of everyone, but I want her prepared. Ben might still try to use it, and I do not want it to catch her off guard."

"He wouldn't dare, you told him of confronting the forger. He must know that the letter will not stand up in any court."

"I wouldn't put it past him to use it just to embarrass her. He just has so much hate toward us! He is his mother's son, through and through. My mother told us so many stories of how mean Antonia was to her and my father."

"It doesn't make any sense. Your mother is the sweetest woman alive. How could anyone hate her?"

"Antonia hated my true grandmother, Gwendolyn. Antonia was jilted by my grandfather because of her. His father made him marry Grandmother Gwendolyn because of her status in the community and her dowry. But he loved Antonia. They must have continued their relationship, or started it up, again at some point, because it was only three weeks after the death of my grandmother that they married. Antonia had a life-long hate for my then seven-year-old father, and then my mother. It was only the fact that she predeceased Theodore that I received the estate as an inheritance. IF, she had survived him, I am sure that she would have found a way to break the trust so that her sons would have inherited."

"Thank God for small favors." She pauses and adds, "But . . . then you would not have moved to EL Dorado, Will would not have lost his Julia, or joined the Army." She shudders. "Life would have been so different. If he wasn't in the Army, he wouldn't have met the little Indian girl that told him that our nephew survived the attack that killed our brother, Ian. We would have never known Joshua's fate." She shudders, again and repeats. "So different!" She pauses.

81

"Grant? You might not have fallen in love with me, if you had seen me grow up instead of seeing me grown for the first time after the years apart." She runs to his side. "I have loved you my whole life and I cried my eyes out when you and Julia moved away. I was only eight, but I adored you, and was heartbroken."

He takes her in his arms. "You never told me that, Carolyn. Why have you kept this a secret these last three years that I have been courting you?"

"I wanted you to think that I was a grown-up falling in love, instead of a schoolgirl who had a crush. That is why, I don't think if you stayed, you would have fallen in love with me. You had to see me as a woman, not watch me grow from a girl. I am not explaining right."

"I think I understand what you are saying, but I disagree with you. Look at your brother. He watched Julia grow to be a woman and loved her through it."

"But he let her leave, instead of proposing to her."

"Oh, I see what you are saying. I would have made the same mistake? No, I still don't agree with your presumption. You were only fourteen, when I first saw you again. You were still a child. I was twenty-four, but I saw the woman that I would love in that almost grown child. I don't think that I would have thought any different if I had watched you go from ten to eleven to twelve etc. I think we were meant to be, whether I stayed or left. You are the only woman for me, and I would have known it when the time was right, either way."

"Are you sure?"

"So sure that I am willing to prove it."

"How can you do that?" She laughs

"By proving how much I love you now. By marrying you again."

"That doesn't prove that you would have loved me if you didn't move."

"It will prove that I will love you my whole life. It would have started at some point, whether I moved or stayed. You are *the* woman I will love forever and ever, amen. Now enough of these 'what ifs'. It is the way it is and I am the luckiest man alive. I need coffee, let's get to Grandmother's. I am hankering for her chicory brew!"

—

**82**

\*\*\*

Mary, Grant and Grandfather Clyde were sitting in their kitchen, while Carolyn was getting fitted.

"That is the most absurd story that I have ever heard! Me, having a 'love child' while married to the most wonderful man in the world? Ridiculous! Why didn't you mention this last night?"

"I didn't want to embarrass you in front of the Lewis's. Ben had a forged letter. It had handwriting very close to yours. I didn't have a chance to look at it very long – they took it from me, by force. But it did look authentic. The age and handwriting were very believable. But, I knew it could not be true. Anyone who has ever heard you talk about Father, would know he was your one true love."

"How can I prove it isn't true, if it looked so believable?"

"Thank the Colonel and Chilly. They found the forger, and we paid him to forge another letter, in the same handwriting. It cost me double what Ben paid - one thousand dollars!" Mary gasps and puts her hand over her mouth. Grant continues, "I do not know what I would have done, if the Colonel did not come out to help. He did everything! The lawyers were no help. Clarence and Annabelle found Molly and Sara, but I was at a loss about what to do about them or the letter. Will thought of everything. I dreaded facing you without having a solution. That is the reason I sent the telegram. I was waiting to see the letter he was talking about, and I did not want to look you in the eye until I had an answer. I did not want to mortify you with the thought of facing such a horrendous situation."

Mary gets up, crosses over to Grant, and puts her arms around him from behind. "What a wonderful son! Did you know how close you came to losing Carolyn over that telegram? She was fit to be tied – but with no rope strong enough to hold her down!"

"I knew she would not like it much. She told me that she threatened to cut off her own hair. Thank god, she forgave me!"

Marilyn comes out of the bedroom. "Grant, I hate to cut

**83**

you short, but I need to bring the bride out of the bedroom in her dress. You need to leave, NOW! Carolyn is getting very anxious, that you are going to see her."

Grant immediately stands. "I must be off, it seems. Tell Carolyn, I will meet her at service." He kisses his mother and grabs his overcoat and leaves.

# EIGHTEEN

## Monday, December 18th, 1882 in Lawrence

After rising early again, Carolyn is eager to head off to Grandmother Marilyn's for another fitting. Grant gives her a kiss good-bye. "Must you leave before breakfast?"

"Yes. This should be the last pinning. I hate this part – it is so tedious! Grandmother promised me that yesterday's sewing would be done. We have it just about perfect. My headdress and veil will be the last thing to sew. Your mother has been sewing that, and I want to add special beading to the veil, myself. Wait until you see me. The dress will make me the most beautiful bride for you!"

"It is a shame." He says.

"What is?"

"I most likely will not even see the dress. You take my breath away with just your smile. And I am very sure that you will be all smiles on Saturday. Don't you think?"

"Typical man, all the work to make everything perfect, and you would be just as happy to marry me in a potato sack! Well, I never!" She leans in and gives him a peck on the cheek. "Not only will you notice the dress, but you better let Mother and Grandmother know how much you like it and appreciate all the work that they have done." She loses her smile. "That's an order, husband!"

He loses his smile, also. "Ordering me around, this soon in our married life? I do not know how I feel about this!" He looks down at his feet. Carolyn is surprised by his response.

"Grant, it is a joke! I am sorry. Are you upset with me?" She lifts his head up to look in his eyes. As she does so, he smiles.

"Gotcha!" He bends to give her a kiss. "I will notice everything and thank everyone, I promise."

"Such a silly man." She gives him a small swat on the shoulder. "Life is going to very unpredictable with you, isn't it?"

"Funny, I was thinking the same thing."

Suddenly, Carolyn clutches her belly. "Oh, something isn't right with me." She says, and she bends over to hold onto

**85**

the chair next to her.

"Carolyn, what is it?  Something you ate?"

"I haven't eaten anything today.  No, this seems more like a 'monthly' pain.  I usually don't get those pains.  My sister is the one who has very unpleasant 'monthlies'.  I am sorry, this is more than you need to know.  Can you go get my mother, for me?"  She says, out of breath from the pain.  Her knuckles are white from holding the chair with all her might while bent over.

Grant is out the door immediately.  "Mother Beth?  Mother Beth?  Come quickly, Carolyn needs you."

Beth runs into Carolyn's bedroom.  "Carolyn, what's wrong?"

"Mother, please shut the door."  Grant is standing there helpless, as the door closes on him.

Carolyn's father, William, has come with his wife.  "What seems to be the fuss, Grant?"

"I do not know.  Carolyn was suddenly in terrible pain.  She seemed very upset about it.  She is very strong girl and she suddenly seemed so vulnerable."

"It will do no good worrying.  Come in the kitchen and get some coffee.  My wife will do everything she can.  Come with me."  William puts his arm around Grant's shoulders.  William is taller than Grant by four or five inches.

Grant sits at the table while William pours his coffee.  "Being a husband takes some getting used to.  We are kept in the dark about how our women do some things.  I was never comfortable when Beth told me to leave when she wasn't well.  Men, naturally, want to fix things, but we cannot fix everything.  Sometimes, all we can do is wait.  Do you want some eggs?  I can fry an egg, as well as any woman."

Grant chuckles.  "I cannot eat just yet.  I am too concerned.  The coffee helps.  As does the company."

A half hour passes, as Grant and his father-in-law sit at the kitchen table and talk.  Grant tells him about his racehorse that is about to give birth.  "You remember last year when she won the derby?  I contracted with my good friend who owns the Blue-Ribbon male for stud.  Joan of Arc is ready to foal any day now."  He looks around for anyone listening.  "I want to give the foal to my bride.  She was so excited to stand in the winner's circle when Joan won. I am sure she would love a horse of her own to race."

William sits back in the chair and sips his coffee. "I cannot think of a better wedding present for her. She loves horses so. It will give her something to do, that she can share with you. You are on the way to being a great husband, Grant. I was worried that she was still too young, but she has changed so much since she left. You are good for her."

Beth comes into the kitchen looking grave. "Grant, I have put Carolyn back to bed. She is still in pain. She is asking for you. I am going to get a hot water bottle for her." Grant immediately leaves the room. Beth moves to the sink and pumps some water into a small pot.

Sara comes into the kitchen, and catches Beth at the sink. "Mistress, what do you need? Let me get that for you." She takes the pot from Beth's hands, and takes it to the stove.

"I need to heat the water for a hot water bottle." Beth is in the cabinet under the wash basin. "I know it is here somewhere. Ah! I found it. Sara, please heat that water to just steamy – do not get it to a boil, that will be too hot, okay?"

"Yes, Mistress. I have filled hot water bottles before. Don't you worry. Who is this for?"

"My daughter Carolyn. She is cramping very bad, the poor thing. She never cramps. I'm worried."

"Mistress, is this her first course since being married?" Before Beth can answer, William gets up.

"Okay. I am going to chop wood, or something else useful," he says to himself as he leaves their presence.

Without skipping a beat, Beth says. "This is her first. Do you think that is the reason? It has been so long since I was a newlywed."

"It was that way with my courses. My first time, I hurt so bad, but didn't bleed. Turns out I wuz with child, my Antonia. I had no idea that wuz how it works, sometimes. Maybe Missus Carolyn is with child, already."

"They have only been married ten days."

"If she is due for her monthly, this might be the tell. Ma-am. I think the water is ready."

In Carolyn's room, Grant is kneeling at her bedside. "Darling, is it any better?"

"A bit, laying down has given me some relief. Mother will be bringing me a hot water bottle. That always helps Margie."

At the doorway comes a voice. "And you always gave me a hard time during my courses. You always thought I was faking the pain for attention." Marjorie has her hands on her hips, and is shaking her head from side to side. "I wouldn't wish them on my enemy, but now you know what I have been going through."

"I will never doubt you again, sister."

Grant stands. "So, not making light of it, but that is what we think it is? Just her courses, coming down? I don't want to see you in pain, darling, but that is a relief for me. I was imagining the worst."

Beth comes bustling through the doorway. "I have your hot water bottle. Grant, why don't you make yourself useful. William is chopping wood. Or why don't you go visit the Colonel. We women will take good care of your wife."

Grant bends down to kiss his bride. "Is that what you would have me do? I am not squeamish about these things. I do not mind staying at your side to help."

"And that is why I love you. No, I have Mother and my sister to attend me, it is not necessary for you to be subjected to my woman's issues. I am sure if I have a problem in Lawrence, I will welcome your assistance."

"God forbid!" He says. "I do not want a repeat of this, ever. If I will take my leave, do not hesitate to call for me." Carolyn shakes her head no. "I insist, Carolyn. You do not have to be brave or think that I do not want to be here for you. I love you, and I am very concerned."

"All right, dear, message received. Now go, and let my mother attend me. I will call for you in a while. I promise. I do not want you away from me for any length of time since I am finally yours."

"Good." He says as he bends down to place a kiss on her forehead. "Now listen to your mother. I will go tell Grandmother that you will not be coming for that fitting." He goes to the doorway. "Is there anything else I can do for you?"

Before Carolyn answers, Beth says. "Ask Marilyn to come, and give us a hand, please. She is a very wise woman in these matters."

"Of course, I will bring her here straight away."

After he leaves, Beth closes the door behind him. "Carolyn, is this the normal time for your bleed?"

"No, actually, I would be a week early. I expected it to come down *ON* my wedding day. That is one of the reasons that when Grant said he wanted to marry in EL Dorado, I jumped at the chance. I did not want our first night together, to be during my course." She says this hesitantly, blushing beyond her hair, and looking at her hands, not being able to make eye contact with her mother.

Margie laughs, "Carolyn, you are a bold one. I would have never thought of that!"

"Be that as it may, ahem. Have you started bleeding? Or is it just the pain?"

"I have not felt any flow, yet. I had just a spot or two. Why? Does that mean, something?"

"Sara was just telling me that when she was pregnant with Antonia, she cramped at the time of each course, and just a few spots of blood during her term. You might be with child, my dear."

"Oh, mother, so soon? I was hoping to have Grant to myself for a year, at least."

"Only time will tell. Stay in bed. When your Grandmother comes, I will have her examine you. Your sister Lizzie will be arriving on Wednesday. She can help, if you still need it. I am so proud of having a daughter who is a doctor."

Marjorie quips, "So you keep saying!"

They all laugh. "Sorry, girls, I am not comparing you, but . . . she has made such a difference for women everywhere. She has helped Julia tremendously. Wichita is close to EL Dorado. You will be able to see her professionally, if need be."

"I wish we had time to see her when Grant and I went there, last weekend. We never left the Bridal Suite." Carolyn realizes that she admitted intimate details, and blushes, again.

\*\*\*

After Grant dropped Marilyn off at the Lewis home, he turns down the road to the Colonel's to visit him and his sister Julia. He did want to see how Molly was doing with her new

**89**

living arrangements and assignments.

Molly answered the door, and was all smiles for him. "I cannot thank you, enough for what you'ze done for Sara and me. She loves working for Mistress Beth as much as I love Missus Julia." She realizes that she is blocking his entrance. "Oh, I am so sorry Master Grant. Please come in." She steps to the side to let him pass. "The Colonel and Missus Julia are at table having some late breakfast. Can I'z get you somthin'? Some bacon or eggs? I'z got new corn bread just come out of the oven. I made fresh butter, yesterday. The little kitchen here iz so nice to work in. Our stove didn't work too well. The bottom was rusted out, and the smoke would sometimes fill the cabin."

"Good thing there was a hole in your roof, you had a natural venting system." He says as he enters the house.

"Master Grant that is very clever! I am so glad that you do not hold your uncle's schemin', agin me."

"I know it wasn't your idea, and that he had you trapped in a situation that you could not escape." He gets to the kitchen. "Good morning, Will. Good morning, Sis. How are you both this morning?" He bends to kiss his sister's cheek.

"Good morning, Grant. We are fine. Is Carolyn with you?" The Colonel stands to shake his hand. "What's the matter? Is something wrong?"

Molly has a cup of coffee for him, and he sits down at the table, and puts his head between his hands. "Carolyn is not well, at all. She says it is her course coming down, but she said that she has never had cramping with it before. I am worried for her. She is normally very strong, and this has her very weak and vulnerable. I am not used to seeing her like that. Mother Beth asked that Grandmother examine her. I am worried that it is something more."

"Colonel, do you mind if I go attend my sister? You can visit with Grant while I go see if I can help. Grant, don't worry, please. She is in good hands, and, of course, Dr. Lizzie will be here on Wednesday."

Will interrupts. "Grant, I was going out to check the fences. Would you join me? It will take your mind off your troubles. I would like to go talk with my neighbor Jeremiah Jessup about buying his property. It is adjacent just to the south, and I would like to build our new house on it. With Molly and her son, we've outgrown this set-up. I wasn't as lucky as you to inherit a mansion."

"No, but I bet you will get there soon." They are all putting on their coats. "Shall we drop Julia off, before we head out?"

Twenty minutes later, they are knocking on the door of Jeremiah Jessup. The homestead is just a dilapidated rickety lean-to. The structure was built quickly after the Massacre in 1863, when his multi-room home was burned to the ground. Jeremiah himself is just as rundown as his house is. He is an old man, close to eighty. He is very short, and wearing tattered clothing. Will starts the conversation. "Good morning, Jeremiah. You remember Mary's son Grant? How are you today?"

"Hello, Will. Howdy, Grant." He looks behind him, and closes the door slightly to try to hide something. "I did not expect you today. I think I have changed my mind. I do not know what will become of me, if I sell." He rubs his scraggly chin, as if in thought. "My son thinks I can get more money than you are offering. I, um . . . am going over my options."

"Jeremiah? Johnny said that you can get more? Did he say that to you in a letter? When was the last time he was here? Does he know the current condition of the place? I do not mind negotiating a little. What was he thinking it was worth? Can we come in, and discuss it further?" The Colonel pushes open the door, and cries out in astonishment. "I do not believe this -- Ben Johnson! What the hell are you doing here? How do you know Jeremiah?"

"I saw the listing, and knew it was a property next to yours. I figured that it was fair game to take property from you since your interference took property from me."

Grant steps forward and speaks up. "Your problem is with me, UNCLE. Not my brother-in-law or his family."

"I will take my victories where I can get them."

Will turns to his neighbor. "Jeremiah, what has he offered you for this land. Doesn't the fact that we have been good neighbors to you over the years count for anything? We have come to your aid many times. We have even planted your crop for you, three times in the same number of years. We did not ask for any compensation, did we?" Jeremiah shakes his head.

"No. We did it because we are good neighbors. This man is a blackmailer, extortionist, and a forger. He has falsely accused my brother-in-law AND his mother Mary of some heinous things. Please do not seriously consider his offer."

"What did he try to do to your mother Mary?" He looks to Grant, but doesn't wait for an answer. "She is the sweetest woman around. Such a beauty! If only, I was 30 years younger, I would have tried to court her." He looks at Ben Johnson. "You need to leave! Your offer is no longer being considered. That poor sweet thing! Mary is a breath of spring air, and you want to make trouble for her? Get out of my house, and off my property!! Colonel, he isn't moving, please show him to the door!"

The Colonel and Grant take a step forward to approach Ben. He holds his hand up. "Fine, it was worth trying. I am leaving." He stands, and looks to Grant. "I will not back down. I promise to keep showing up where you least expect it, and make your life as miserable as I can." He doesn't wait for a response, but just walks out the door.

Poor old Jeremiah sits down, and pulls a dirty kerchief from the top pocket of his bib overalls. His hand is shaking. "Sorry, Will, I did not know. He was offering me so much more than you had. I was blinded by my greed. I would never do anything against Mary. Not in a million years. Not for a million dollars!"

Will crosses the room. "Not to worry, Jeremiah. No harm done! I will try to make it up to you. I can raise my offer by a couple of hundred dollars, if that helps."

"No, Will. You met my asking price. His was not a legitimate offer." He stands up, crosses to Will, and holds out his hand. "We have a deal. When do you want to sign the papers? I do not have much to move out of here, but Johnny said that he will come home and help pack me up. The land is yours. I did not plant a cover crop this year, like I usually do. But it should be fertile enough, come spring."

"That will be perfect, Jeremiah. We can sign the papers at any time. I will not take possession until spring. I do want to build a house on the hill overlooking everything, so you can stay in this one, as long as you need or want – free of charge."

"You are more than generous, Will. Thank you."

\*\*\*

After they look over the fences, they head back to the Lewis home. Carolyn is feeling better, and is sitting in the living room with Julia holding her hand. Both women are smiling as if a big secret is being shared.

Grant rushes to his wife's side. "You look so much better, my dear. I am so relieved." He kneels on the floor, opposite of where his sister is sitting, and takes Carolyn's hand.

"Yes, dear, I am feeling much better. Grandmother was even able to bring my dress over, so that we were able to get that fitting in, after all." She cannot stop smiling.

"Not that I am complaining, but why are you smiling like this?"

Julia gets off the seat. "Grant, sit next to your wife." She goes to her husband, puts her arm on his, and says, "Let's give them a moment of privacy, dear." The Colonel lets her lead him into the kitchen without comment.

"What is it, Carolyn?"

"It is actually too early to know for sure, but there is the good possibility that I am going to have a baby."

"Already? Didn't you think that your course was starting?"

"I am not bleeding. I am a week early for it. Sara said that she cramped without bleeding every time her monthly was due; the whole time she was pregnant with Antonia. I am going to be on modified bed rest until I know either way." She looks down at the hand holding hers. "This is quite a shock. I wanted to have you all to myself for a year or so, but I am very excited, too. Giving you a child would be the best wedding present, don't you think?

"It sort of matches my own." He smiles, and gives her a kiss on the cheek.

She looks at him blankly. "What does that mean?"

"Joan of Arc is about to give birth. I have kept it a secret because I wanted to give the new foal to you as a wedding present." He puts his arms around her. "I give you a newborn and you give me one, too.  We are so perfectly matched.  It is like it was meant to be!"

# NINETEEN

## Tuesday, December 19th, 1882 in Lawrence

Carolyn wakes with no Grant beside her. This was the first time in eleven days that she has opened her eyes alone. "Grant?" She calls out.

The door opens to her small bedroom, and Grant walks in, still in his robe, holding a tray with coffee and a warm biscuit for her. "I am right here, my dear. Did you sleep well?"

"What is this? Breakfast in bed? Put the tray on the dresser and come here, my husband."

"Carolyn, I think that we should hold off . . . you know, until we are sure you are not with child or we are sure the child is secure in your womb." He puts the tray down and kneels next to her to plant a kiss on her forehead. "Are we in any pain, this morning?"

"None. Do you think such a precaution is necessary? I am feeling good as new."

"I had a very embarrassing discussion with Will last evening. He said that your sister Lizzie recommended abstinence each time Julia thought she was carrying. I love you too much to harm you or our baby. So, yes. I feel it is absolutely necessary."

Carolyn pretends to pout. "That is why I wanted to hold out, to have you for myself for the first year. I am not tired of you yet." She now smiles up at him. "But it is as God wills it. Bring me that biscuit, please, I am just starving."

As he watches her devour her biscuit, he adds, "Will also suggested that we hire your family's attorneys to file a 'Cease and Desist' order against Uncle before he comes up with any other antics. Will is taking me to them this morning. You will behave and take it easy while I am gone?"

She is through with her biscuit in two bites, and while sipping her fresh hot coffee, she swings her legs across the edge of the bed, and comes to a stand. She drains her cup, and hands it back to Grant. "I will come back to bed, or couch as soon as I have more breakfast. I am still very hungry. I could be eating for two, now. Hand me my robe, please."

He puts the cup down on the tray, and holds her robe so that she can put her arms in the sleeves. As she wraps herself, he doesn't let go. His arms are around her from behind. He is a few inches taller than she, so he must bend ever so slightly to kiss her neck behind her ear. "Have I ever told you that I love the taste of your skin, especially in the morning."

"Now stop that, if you want me to behave!" With that warning, she turns to face him and puts her arms around his neck. "I love you too much to be 'good' now that I know what it is like to have you."

"Again, I will say we are perfectly matched in every way." He pulls her arms from around his neck. "I must insist. Go, get more breakfast. I must get dressed. The Colonel is coming to pick me up at nine."

"You don't love me anymore," Carolyn says with her pretend pout. "Eleven days married, and you've become an old stick in the mud."

"Do you want your money back on your purchase?" he plays along.

"No . . . I will ride out this storm and pray for sunshine ahead." Her stomach loudly grumbles. "I'd love to continue this discussion, but I need to get to the breakfast table before Chilly, or there will be nothing left to eat."

\*\*\*

The Colonel and Grant leave the lawyer's office. Grant says, "They were at least helpful compared to *MY* lawyers. Mine refused to be proactive, at all." Grant says as he is lifting himself onto the buggy seat. "I am so glad that you thought of this. It should get Ben's attention."

"I still cannot believe the nerve of him, going to Jeremiah's like that. I do not trust him to not try to get Molly, again. He does not seem to understand the word NO."

"I feel like I am waiting for the other shoe to fall. Waiting to see what he will try next. This might help."

The Colonel gets in the buggy next to him. He is taller than Grant by six inches. He is looking over his head at the livery. Isn't that Thornton's horse?"

Grant turns to look. "I didn't pay much attention to his

horse. It could be. What could they be trying to do now?"

"Let's sit here for a minute. I want to see who's the rider. If it is Thornton, I might just have a plan."

They sit for forty minutes. Though the sun is out, the temperature is quite chilly. Grant is shivering in his light overcoat. The Colonel gives him a hard time.

"You do not know cold until you are out in it for days at a time. I had too much of it in the cavalry, chasing the Cheyenne and looking for Joshua."

Just as Grant is about to say he gives up; Thornton comes out of the diner, and walks to his horse. His head is down, and he doesn't look around to see the buggy or its occupants. As Thornton kicks his horse to move, the Colonel grabs the reins and stays a distance behind him.

Before long, Thornton comes to the end of Massachusetts Ave. The Colonel knows that this means he is headed out of town.

"We cannot let him leave. We need to question him." He gives a 'Hiyaa!' to the horses and cracks the whip over their heads, and they take off running. It takes a few moments before they catch up with him. The Colonel guesses his next move, and takes the road that he knows will intersect with Thornton's just a little way down. Within a few minutes they are waiting at the intersection for him to catch up. "Here he comes." The Colonel warns. He calls to the horses, "Hiyaa!" Just as he goes to cross the road, the Colonel's buggy blocks his way, and Thornton must come to an abrupt stop. The Colonel grabs his rifle, jumps down, and is at Thornton's side before he even recognizes the duo. "Well, Thornton. I thought you'd be long gone by now. What are you still doing in town?"

"Wouldn't you like to know?" Thornton tries to move his horse. Grant is down, also and has gone on the other side of the horse and has a hold of the reins. "Let go, Grant! I am not going to tell you anything!"

Grant has a strong hold, and Thornton's attention is moved back to the Colonel at the sound of the rifle cocking. "Get down, Thornton. We need to talk."

Thornton reluctantly gets off his horse, giving both men an evil stare. "I have nothing to say."

"Let me ask you a question, then. How much is Ben

**97**

paying you?" The Colonel gives him a wink.

"Why would you ask me that?"

"Because we'd like to make you an offer that you'd be a fool to refuse."

"What kind of offer?"

"Answer his question, first." Grant says as he leads the horse to the buggy, and ties the reins to a side rail.

"Ben is paying me $10 a month." He says with great pride and a smile.

Will walks over to Grant and they talk a moment.

The Colonel lowers the rifle a bit. "He'd like to pay you an additional $10 to match the amount that you are receiving from Ben and give you a $2 to $5 bonus for each report of Ben's activities, whether you think they have something to do with Grant or not."

"So I will still work for Ben?"

The Colonel rolls his eyes and explains further. "You will need to keep close to Ben, and help him more than ever. You just need to inform Grant of any doings that might affect him and his ownership on the Johnson estate."

"You want me to be a spy?"

The Colonel answers, "Yes, but you will be a double agent for good instead of evil."

"Only if *he* is smart enough to handle it." Grant adds, "I am having some doubts."

The Colonel walks over to Thornton, and puts his arm over his shoulder. "Come on, Thornton. Let's make Grant feel better about this. Give us a sample of a bonus item. You'd be a far richer man, for it. I promise. Where is Ben now, and what is he up to next?"

# TWENTY

## Wednesday, December 20ᵗʰ, 1882 in Lawrence

Carolyn hasn't lifted a finger to help with any of the physical last-minute details for her wedding that is only three days away.  She has been working on the beading for her veil.  She is sewing in her mother's room so that Grant knows not to walk in on her.  Her mother has a beautiful lounge chair that was a thirty-fifth wedding anniversary present from her very thoughtful father. Carolyn is sewing prayers into her head covering.  She is praying that she is going to have a baby and that all the troubles in EL Dorado will work itself out.

Her grandmother Marilyn has brought the dress over for the final fitting.  She walked over, and the December weather was much colder today than it's been.  Carrying the heavy satin wedding dress, and breathing the cold air has left her out of breath when she finally reached the Lewis household.  Beth was very worried.  "Mother, you should not have walked over, you should have taken a buggy in this weather."

"Pish-Posh!  Much ado about nothing.  I just need to catch a breath."  She looks around the room.  "Is the groom gone?  We do not want him to see this."

As Beth was going to answer, Grant and the Colonel rush into the house.  Marilyn hurriedly covers up the dress with the bag that she carried it in, while Beth says, "My, my, what is all the fuss?  I thought you boys were going to spend the day, mending fences together."

Will explains.  "Grant just received a telegram from his lawyers in EL Dorado.  A suit has been filed to attest the trust. I cannot believe Ben will not let this go!"

Beth's husband William comes into the room to hear the news.  "Didn't Ben get the Cease and Desist order?"  He asks.

"This must have been filed the same day as the Order we had drawn up," Grant answers.  "This is just going to drag my mother's good name in the mud.  He is just trying to hurt us, anyway that he can."

Carolyn comes into the room from her parents' room. "What are we to do?"

Grant goes to his bride. "I am so sorry to darken this joyous occasion with my family problems."

The Colonel answers, "We are all family, Grant. Your problems are OUR problems. Haven't you noticed?"

"I know, but I feel like I have brought a burden on you all."

"Poppycock!" Carolyn says as her mother and grandmother gasp. "Ben Johnson is the one burdening us. I just hope we can get him to understand that we will not back down."

"In the meantime, Carolyn, we need to put this dress on you. Grant – I don't mean to be rude, but get out of here!" grandmother Marilyn says with authority.

The women all go into Beth's room, and help Carolyn into her dress. It is just perfect. It has a high collar, but only lace on the shoulders. Carolyn's bosom is lifted high and her waist is very slim. The satin base is delicately covered in lace, and has many beautiful white pearls in a floral pattern. Her train is four feet long, and edged also in white pearls. Beth starts crying at the sight of her beautiful daughter. "Shall we try on the veil with it?" She asks.

"No, no. I do not want the whole thing put together until THE day. Grandmother, you have done an outstanding job!"

There is a knock on the bedroom door, and a small voice says, "Darling, may I come in and see?" Without waiting for an answer, Mary opens the door slightly and squeezes in. "Oh, Carolyn!" is all she can say before her tears take over. "So beautiful! I am so happy for my son. HE is so in love with you. You know that, don't you? That nonsense with the telegram had nothing to do with his feelings for you." Mary crosses the room, and takes Carolyn's hands. "How are you feeling? Any more pain?"

"I am fit as a fiddle, and just as in love and happy as my husband seems to be. We would be thrilled if I am with child, already. Could we be so lucky, so soon?"

"I pray that it is so." She lets go of Carolyn's hands, and walks around the dress. "Have you put the train up, yet?"

"Not yet." Marilyn, Beth and Carolyn all say at the same time, then laugh. They all reach for the long bottom of the dress, and start putting it up into the hooped bustle.

Once everything is buttoned into place and nothing is touching the floor, Carolyn begins her swirling around. She suddenly stops, and puts her hand to her belly. "I almost forgot."

"Are you in pain?" Marilyn asks.

"No, but I do not want to take any chances. Let's get this beautiful perfect dress off, and let me rest. I am too excited and full of energy, but I have work to do on my veil still, and that will calm me down."

Beth is unbuttoning her and says, "You have matured overnight, my girl. You have a good head on your shoulders."

"She is going to be the best wife and mother!" Mary adds.

Beth looks at the clock on her dresser. "Oh, it is almost time to get Lizzie from the train!! I cannot wait to see her. Three years is too long an absence for a mother and her child. No matter how old they are!"

***

Margie, Chilly and Beth go into Lawrence to meet Lizzie. Dr. Lizbet Lewis has been a gynecologist in Wichita for a few years. She has dark blonde wavy hair, but is very petite like her mother Beth. She is in her in her late twenties, and married to her work. When she walks down the first step off the train, she turns back and smiles at a man behind her. He smiles back at her and hurries to meet her on the step to take her elbow and help her down. She sees her siblings and mother, and waves wildly at them. They all rush to her, and take turns hugging her. Beth hugs her twice.

"Oh, it is so nice to have my girl home. Did you have a nice travel, dear?" Beth says to Lizzie, but is looking at the gentleman next to her.

"It was lovely, Momma. Let me introduce you to my friend. This is Dr. Ezra Scott. He works with me in Wichita, and has a brother here in Lawrence. He is a dear, dear friend. He will be my date to Carolyn's wedding. Ezra, this is my mother Beth, my little sister Marjorie, and my baby brother, Chilly." They shake hands all around.

Beth talks first. "It is very nice to meet you, and we are

**101**

glad to have you at the wedding. Sorry, Carolyn could not come to meet you herself, she is feeling under the weather, and we are keeping a close eye on her."

"Is there anything I can do?" Ezra offers.

Beth blushes, "I think our Lizzie will be needed in this area, but thank you for your offer. What is your specialty?"

"I am a gynecologist, also. But, you are right, having her sister attend her is all she will need. Lizzie can consult with me if she feels it is necessary." Ezra is a short man, but taller than Lizzie and Beth by three or four inches. He sees his brother and says, "Pardon me, but my brother has arrived for me." He steps over to Lizzie, and gives her a kiss on the cheek. "May I call on you tonight? Or tomorrow?" He blushes.

"You may do both, if you like. You can join the family for supper, if I might be so bold as to ask."

"I am not sure what my brother has planned. He is a bachelor. I have not seen him in two years, but . . ."

Lizzie does not let him finish. "Bring him with you, the more the merrier. Right, Momma?"

"Absolutely! Please ask him to join us." Encourages Beth. "Is he an older brother or younger?"

Ezra looks at Marjorie. "He is my baby brother. So, I imagine dinner with him would not be home cooked."

"All the more reason to join us." Lizzie says.

Beth looks to her son. "Chilly take Lizzie's bags to the buggy, please." Chilly leaves with her bag. "Ezra go ask your brother if he has plans. It would be so nice for you to be there for Lizzie."

"Thank you, Mrs. Lewis. I will be right back." Ezra walks to the man waiting in the buggy. They shake hands and talk for a moment or two. Ezra hurries back. "We would be delighted to join you for supper. Emmet says he knows where your farm is located. What time shall we call, and do you need us to bring anything?"

Beth says, "How sweet of you to offer, but we have everything we need. Dinner will be at 7:30."

"I wouldn't miss it." He goes to Lizzie, and gives her another kiss on the cheek. "See you then, sweetheart." He says in a very low voice.

As soon as he leaves, Marjorie grabs Lizzie's arm. "Tell

us everything! How long have you known him? How long have you've been courting? Why haven't you told us anything about him in your letters?"

Lizzie is blushing as she answers, "I have worked with him for years. When he mentioned not seeing his brother for a while, I suggested accompanying me to Lawrence. On the train, we . . . um . . . got much closer. I have admired him for quite some time, but he has never given me any indication that he felt the same way. Until the lovely train ride!"

Chilly comes back to the group and butts in. "How can a train ride be 'lovely'?"

All three women laugh. Lizzie looks at her brother who stands seventeen inches taller than her. "You are, obviously, too little to understand?" Once again, all three women laugh.

"How am I little?" Chilly says as he stands even taller than before.

Beth grabs his hand, and gives it a pat. "It was lovely because of the company she shared."

Marjorie says, "We need to get Chilly a girlfriend."

"Don't you dare! I saw what a girl has done to Will and Grant. They are whipped! Sorry, I want to see stuff. I am going to join the cavalry when I am seventeen. Someday, I would like to be a sheriff of a small town. But, not until I see more of this great country. I would like to find Harkahome, and spend some time with him and his tribe. I want adventure."

"I would love to know how Joshua and Lydia are doing. I sure hope they do not regret staying with the Cheyenne." Beth says. Her grandson Joshua and his mother Lydia have been living with the Cheyenne since the Massacre in Oberlin, Kansas in 1878. That is where her son Ian was killed. Joshua's Cheyenne name is Harkahome. Lydia's name is JaUne.

Lizzie interrupts her mother's thoughts. "What is going on with Carolyn. She is unwell?"

"She feels fine, now. She is just being cautious." Margie offers. They are all climbing into the buggy. "We can tell you more when delicate ears are not listening." She gives her brother a shove.

"Nothing about me is delicate! They don't want to say it in front of me, but they are thinking she might be pregnant."

**103**

He says in a very offhanded way.

"Chilly! Must you be crude?" Beth swats at him.

"Geez, Momma. Lizzie is a doctor, and she has heard the word 'pregnant' before. We all have. What is the big deal?"

"It is just not polite talk in mixed company." Explains Beth.

"I think I must borrow Carolyn's word – Poppycock!" Chilly shoots back. "I am her brother – not company! I just do not understand all these crazy rules. Women can talk amongst themselves about this, but have a man add to the conversation, and it is impolite?"

Lizzie is nodding her head. "I agree with Chilly. I work with women all the time, and the men are kept from hearing or knowing what the diagnosis is because it is impolite to discuss. It is very frustrating trying to convince a woman to confide in her husband. How can he help if he doesn't know what is going on? Men are supposed to be the stronger sex, but they cannot hear what a woman – the weaker sex – goes through to bear them children? None of it makes sense to me."

"Spoken like a thoroughly modern woman," Beth says. "Lizzie, when we get home, talk with Carolyn in private; we are all concerned for her."

"Of course, Mother. Little Carolyn is married with a possible babe on the way. I helped deliver her. I feel so old."

"I know the feeling," adds Beth.

***

Before dinner, Lizzie examines Carolyn, and says that it is too early to tell if she is with child. She proclaims her healthy, and said that she can resume normal activities. Carolyn leans in and asks in a whisper, "All activities?" Then she blushes.

"I think you will be fine. You haven't had cramps in forty-eight hours so . . . I cannot see making Grant suffer by not being a full husband to you. I know how important these things are with newlyweds."

Carolyn blushes again. "It is wonderful. I never knew how much I would enjoy myself . . . in bed! Grant is so sweet and loving. Do many women say that?"

**104**

"No, they don't usually talk about it, but I've known it can be great, just being around Mother and Father while they were busy conceiving each of you. I think it depends on the man, and the love the couple feel for each other. I hear that many men just do it, and do not take their wife's needs into consideration. I am glad that Grant is not one of those."

Carolyn blushes again. "He is more than considerate. Let me just say that! Will it change if I am with child?"

"It will be different as your body changes. There will still be ways to meet each other's needs no matter how big you get. If you have a normal pregnancy, you can have relations the whole time. He can't hurt the growing baby by being in you, just remember that."

"I wish you could deliver my babies, Lizzie. I wish Wichita and EL Dorado were closer."

"It is easy to figure out your due date, though babies have a mind of their own on when to be born. I can take a week off before and after your date, so that I can deliver him or her. We might be rushing this whole discussion, though. We should know within the next three weeks. Some women are late their first month of marriage just due to the activity there. You say you've been regular like a clock for two years, but you are using your body differently now."

"I'll say!" She blushes yet again.

\*\*\*

Roast beef and fried chicken will be served for dinner. It is a full house, and Beth was very glad for all of Sara's delicious cooking. Molly came to help cook and serve, also. There are fourteen expected for dinner. It will be Grandfather Clyde, and Grandmother Marilyn; William and Beth, of course; Lizzie, her Ezra and his brother Emmet; the Colonel and his Julia; Grant and Carolyn; Marjorie invited her suitor Richard Long; and last, but not least, Chilly will be there to entertain. Dinner lasts two hours, they eat slowly, and laugh heartily until they find themselves unable to move.

Both Emmet Scott and Richard Long are very attentive to Marjorie. Emmet is taller than his brother, but it doesn't matter since Marjorie isn't taller than her sister, Lizzie. Emmet is only twenty-one years old.  Ezra just turned thirty.

After the table is cleaned and everyone has moved to the parlor, Carolyn goes to the pianoforte, and sits down.  "Shall we sing some Christmas Carols?  Marjorie comes to her side and says, "I guess I will give you your Christmas present, early.  Wait here."  She goes into her bedroom, and brings out some papers and gives them to her baby sister.  "I know how you love this new song, so I bought you the sheet music.  Do you think you can play it?"  Carolyn looks at the music sheet, and stands and hugs her sister.  "You know me, so well.  This is my favorite!  Give me a minute to go over this.  Will you sing this with me?"  She sits back down, already reading the notes on the page.

"I am not the singer you are.  I don't want to ruin it.  You are better as a soloist."  She bends down and gives her taller sister a kiss on the forehead.

Carolyn runs through the song once, while she hums along.  She smiles, then starts the song for all to hear.

> "Away in the Manger
> No Crib for HIS bed
> The little Lord Jesus
> Laid down his sweet head.
>
> The stars on the bright sky
> Looked down where HE lay
> The little Lord Jesus
> Asleep on the hay.
>
> The cattle are lowing
> The poor Baby wakes
> But little Lord Jesus
> No crying He makes.
>
> I love Thee, Lord Jesus
> Look down from the sky
> And stay by my side
> 'Till morning is nigh.
>
> Be near me, Lord Jesus

I ask Thee to stay
Close by me forever
And love me, I pray.

Bless all the dear children
In Thy tender care
And take us to heaven
To live with Thee there.

Grant gets up from his seat and walks to her. It is as if he is metal, and she is the magnet. He is powerfully drawn to her. When she is done with the song, he sits down at her side on the piano bench and takes her hand. "How did God make the most perfect woman mine? How am I worthy?" He drops his chin to his chest. "I am not, but I will spend my life working to be so. I promise." He raises her hand and kisses it. "Please sing more songs. I can listen to you all day." She blushes and kisses him back and whispers. "Go sit down over there. I cannot concentrate on the keys, with you this close."

Beth watches all her children with their mates or suitors, and she is glad that they each have found the happiness that she and William have shared for thirty-six years. She can tell that Carolyn will be very happy with Grant, as is Will with his Julia. It may be too soon to tell for Lizzie, but she can see that Ezra adores her and she him. Richard Long has been courting Margie since the Colonel's ball, and he doesn't seem to like the competition Emmet is giving for her affection.

At the end of the evening, Emmet and Ezra are the first to leave. Emmet manages to pull Margie aside, and ask her if she was available for lunch and a ride in the country on Sunday.

"I am not sure, Emmet. The big wedding is Saturday, and we will have family in town for the Holidays. My brother Joseph and his family are coming in tomorrow, but will not leave until Monday. Do you mind if we wait until next weekend?" She and Emmet both see Richard coming toward them.

Emmet bows to her. "As you wish, a week from Sunday it is. I will pick you up at one, then?"

**107**

"I would like that very much."

"Then have a great visit with your family. I will see you then." Emmet nods to Richard, takes his coat from Chilly, thanks Beth for dinner, and leaves with Ezra. Richard is standing next to Margie as he watches Emmet leave.

Margie says, "Richard, are you leaving also?"

"I was hoping to talk to you for a minute."

"What about?"

"I wanted to ask you to the New Year's Eve dance. I had so much fun dancing with you at the Colonel's ball. Please say you'll go with me?" He looks nervously at her.

"I would love a chance to dance with you again. I hadn't heard about this dance. I guess we are so tied up in the wedding preparations to be aware of anything else. Which day is it? Saturday?"

"Well, no. New Year's Eve is Sunday."

"Oh, of course it is. What time is the dance?"

"Eight o'clock. I was hoping to take you out to dinner first. I could pick you up at six?"

Before Margie can answer, she tries to figure out if she has enough time to get home from lunch with Emmet, and get ready for dinner and a dance. She ends up counting the hours on her fingers. "Yes, Richard, I will be ready at six. Of course, we will be dancing at Carolyn's wedding. Won't you get tired of me after that?"

"Never, Margie. I know that you will be very busy with family the next few days, so I will see you at the wedding." He bends down, and gives her a kiss on the cheek. "I cannot wait, my dear, until then." He takes his coat from Chilly, and leaves.

Once it was just the family together, Chilly approaches Will and says, "Who do you think will win Margie's heart?"

Will smiles at his younger sister. "Chilly, I think that Richard will win Margie, hands down and soon. Emmet doesn't have a chance. Sorry, Lizzie, I know you are sweet on Ezra, but his brother has come into the picture a few weeks too late."

Marjorie blushes. "How you talk about me as if I am not here. How do you know that I might not like Emmet more? I will be seeing him next Sunday."

"The dance is Sunday. How are you going to see them both?" Chilly asks.

"Emmet asked me to lunch at one, and a drive afterward. If I am home by four, I will have enough time to get ready for my date with Richard."

Will leans in close to Margie, "My only advice to you is: don't call the one by the other's name on Sunday. That could make things a little tricky." Chilly starts laughing, and cannot stop.

Marjorie is not amused. She gets up, and says, "Laugh all you want, Chilly. At least I have someone interested in me. Who are you taking to the wedding or the dance? You need to start looking at the opposite sex, you are sixteen. Really, what are you waiting for?"

"I told you this afternoon, I am not interested in getting into any relationship. I am going into the cavalry."

"Against my advice!" says Will. "He won't listen to me." He turns to his baby brother. "I have until October to turn you around, and I am going to do my best to talk you out of this, Chilly."

"You'll be wasting your breath, Will. This is what I have wanted to do since before I went to school. I remember hearing Father talk about the war. I have always wanted to be in uniform, just like he was, and you were."

"There is much more to it than just the uniform! We have had many discussions about my days in service, and I have told you that if I had to do it all over again, I would have chosen a different path."

"So you say. I have the right to find out for myself. Just like you did, big brother."

Beth walks into the room. "Do you remember how I was when Will was gone? Do you want to put me through that again?"

"We all know that Will has always been your favorite. You won't worry as much for me. I am not signing up during any outbreaks of hostilities. Will has already trained me for the hardships. I learned how to find my way through the wilderness and rough terrain. I am going into this so much more aware of what is to be expected of me than he did. And I am smarter, and better looking to boot!" He smiles like the kid who just swallowed the forbidden candy. That smile always makes Beth melt.

She walks to where he is sitting, and messes up his red hair. "I think that is enough discussion about this for one night. I need to get some rest. Joseph and his family are coming in the morning on the nine o'clock train. I am going to bed. The next several days are going to take all my strength. Do not wear me down with this talk of leaving, I beg of you. All of you." Now she is looking at the Colonel.

"I didn't start it. Marjorie did." He smiles, and crosses the room to his mother, and bends to kiss her forehead. "Go, rest, Mother. We will not talk of it any more. Julia and I will head home now, but we will see you early tomorrow."

# TWENTY-ONE

## Thursday, December 21ˢᵗ, 1882 in Lawrence

Joseph, Katherine, and their two little ones, Samuel and Constance, are met at the train by Will and Julia, and brought directly to Legacy Plantation.

Constance is a just two months old. Samuel is in two, and has wreaked havoc on the train ride. He is too full of energy now to sit still in the buggy. Beth is thrilled that Katherine has been so good about traveling with her newborns. When Samuel was barely a few months old, they traveled in for the holidays then also.

Beth is waiting for them on the porch. She runs to the buggy. "Oh, I have my whole family home!! Samuel, come to Grandma." The little one is very reluctant to go to her. "Come on, little one, Grandma loves you, and I have fresh baked cookies for you in the kitchen." This gets him to go with her. She takes him by the hand, and leads him into the house.

Carolyn comes out of the house in time to be able to take her new niece Connie, as her parents have come to call her. "Oh, she is so precious!" She looks to her older brother. "Do I see red wisps of hair starting? Welcome to my ginger world, little girl. Thank God she looks like you, Katherine. She is so beautiful!" Carolyn carries her into the house. "Mother, look! She is going to be a red-head!"

"God help us!" Joseph says. "The only question is - will she be like fire or ice?" He says quoting from their father regarding the two very different red-heads he had – Carolyn and Chilly.

"She will be fire, like her favorite Auntie!" Responds Carolyn.

Julia speaks up. "You can't claim to be her favorite. She has me and Marjorie and Lizzie. Lizzie has the best chance since she will know her better than any of us."

"Finally, a perk of our business partnership that I will use to my full advantage." Lizzie quips.

The family settles in for a wonderful reunion. Everyone vies for the attention of little Samuel and Connie. At one point in the early afternoon, Beth is standing in the back of the room just watching her large family all together. She becomes teary eyed. Her William sees her, and goes to her side. "I am thinking of Ian, too, Beth. He is still with us."

"He would have loved to see his best friend Joseph's happy little family. They were so close growing up. I wonder how Joshua and Lydia are doing. I pity her life each winter. From what Will has told us, they are tortuous in Wyoming."

"Yes, but they chose that life. Who knows? Lydia might have had more children. And Joshua Nathaniel is almost old enough now to pick a bride from the tribe. Or maybe he will decide to come back to Kansas to see his Gram Beth." He gives her a big hug from behind. "Just continue to keep them all in your thoughts, and your prayers. We may see them again. God willing."

The Colonel sees his parents in the back, and can tell what they are thinking. He has finally gotten a turn at holding little Connie, and he gets up and brings her to his mother. "Only happy tears are allowed during this wonderful homecoming, Mother. Look at this little baby, and all the possibilities that lie ahead of her. Look at all that your love has created." He waves to all his siblings. "And we have many happy years ahead of us all." He hands her Connie and bends to kiss her forehead. "We owe everything to you, Mother. You should be very proud of all you've done."

"I am so proud. I feel I might burst."

There is a knock on the door, and it is Ezra and Emmet. Each holding a bouquet of flowers. Lizzie runs to Ezra. "I am so glad that you've come. Joseph has arrived, and you haven't seen the new baby yet." He hands her the flowers, and bends to kiss her cheek. She blushes and gives him a cheek kiss back. Ezra works with Joseph, but the eldest brother had no idea that Ezra and Lizzie have feelings for each other. He just stares at the two.

Ezra sees the stare and blushes, but goes to him. "Joseph, I would like to introduce my baby brother Emmet." He leans close to Joseph. "He is sweet on Marjorie. I mean, really sweet on her." He looks back at Emmet. "Brother, this is my boss in Wichita. He is Lizzie and Marjorie's older brother, Dr. Joseph Lewis." Joseph shakes his hand, but doesn't smile at

**112**

either brother.

Emmet still has the flowers in his hand. "These are for Marjorie. Is she home?"

"I am right here." Marjorie comes out of the kitchen. "These are beautiful. Thank you, Emmet. You shouldn't have."

"I was wondering, Marjorie, if you'd like to go for a walk with me, and show me the grounds. It is a nice sunny day, and not as cold as it has been. I know that you are visiting with your family, but . . ." He leans close. "I could not stop thinking about you. I understand that I have competition with Richard, but I just wanted you to get to know me. I would like a chance to be your suiter, too. If you'd let me."

"Well, I like that very much. Though, I must admit that I am used to fellas trying to get past *me* to get to *Carolyn.* My little sister has always stolen the show."

"She is a beauty with that red hair, but I prefer curly haired brunettes with giant brown eyes." Again, he leans in. "I could get lost in those eyes."

Margie blushes. "Well, let's go for that walk. You and your brother must stay for dinner again."

"I wouldn't want to impose. You have so many here now with your brother's family."

"It will be just fine, I promise." She leaves his side and goes into the kitchen to put the flowers in water. She tells her mother that she has invited the brothers to supper. "Momma, he says he likes me. Can you believe it? First Richard - now Emmet."

"Of course, I believe it, Marjorie. I was very popular in my day."

William speaks up. "And out of all our children, you look and act most like your mother. And who doesn't love my Beth." Says William.

"Father, I cannot think of a single person." Marjorie admits, beaming proudly.

# TWENTY-TWO

## Friday, December 22nd, 1882 in Lawrence

Grant wakes beside his bride, and waits impatiently for the sigh she makes, before she opens her eyes. He is smiling, watching her sleep for several minutes. He cannot wait any longer and reaches for her face and caresses it. She smiles and her hand moves to take his. With her eyes still closed, she says, "Just a few more minutes, darling. I will wake then."

"But I want you, now." He whispers in her ear.

She sighs, and opens one eye. "Then take me." She holds open her arms for him to come to her.

He hesitates, "Are you sure this will be all right?"

"Lizzie said since I have no cramping, we can resume our activities. Are you going to keep me waiting?"

"Never, my love. I am at your beck and call."

"As I – you." She whispers in his ear before she nibbles on his ear lobe. "It has been too long, take me, now." She kisses him passionately. "Don't stop wanting me if I get fat with our baby. Promise?"

"I promise, only if it is safe to do so."

"Stop talking, and show me how much you love me."

"Yes, my love." He rolls on top of her. "I will never stop wanting you this way." He takes his time, entering her slowly, and then makes sure that she enjoys him, as much as he enjoys her.

Afterward, Carolyn lies in his arms. "Grant, I think tonight you should sleep at Grandmother Marilyn's. I don't want you to see me tomorrow until I walk down the aisle. Will you do that for me?"

"Must I? I do not want to spend a night apart."

"Maybe that is too close to me. Maybe you should sleep at Will and Julia's. I will have the Colonel guard you so that you do not sneak off."

"You are so superstitious! I don't want to spend a night without you, ever!"

"This will be the last one. I promise." She turns to rise.

When she gets up on her side of the bed, she looks back

at him. "There is the exception of Deer Hunting season. I know how fond of that you are. Of course, if we are still without a little one, I can accompany you. I am an excellent shot, if you recall."

"It worries me, how excellent you are. With that temper of yours, I will need to stay on your good side."

"Good, it is settled then. You will stay at Will's tonight! After that, AT MY SIDE, will always be my GOOD SIDE. Agree?"

"Like I have a choice." They are both standing and dressing. She walks over to him and adjusts his collar.

"You have a choice, my darling. Obey me or pay the consequences. Which will it be?"

"Wasn't there something in our vows about love, honor and obey? I think you said those words."

"If you want me to say them again, obey me."

"I can see that I do not have a winning hand in this game. I must long to hold for a whole night or never hold you again."

"See, there is my smart man. Putting all the pieces together. There is so much going on today. We have the rehearsal at the church, then the private dinner at the Colonel's club. It is going to make a gorgeous venue for our wedding. The Lawrence Gun and Sport Club is the most envied wedding location since they opened their doors two years ago. I can peek in the room, to see if they have started the decorations yet. I rented an archway, and . . . well, I won't give it all away. I will let you be surprised by all the beautiful things that I have selected for our wedding. Do you think it will be too much for me to wear the teal ball gown tonight? I was looking forward to standing at the altar in it with you. Sort of a repeat event." She is all smiles.

"It might be too much if no one else will be so attired. Ask Julia or one of our mothers; I would trust their judgment." He is totally dressed and has his hand on the doorknob to exit the room. "Strike that statement. It is your wedding rehearsal, do whatever makes you happy. Everyone who loves you will be happy you did so. Especially me." He doesn't wait for a comment, but opens the door to leave.

Before he takes another step, she grabs his hand, which

surprises him. "Grant, I do not deserve you."

He turns around and moves some of her red hair that is still down and has fallen in her face. "I am the unworthy one, and I will spend my whole life trying to make up for it."

\*\*\*

The morning and afternoon both fly by with the meals, and organizing the activities of the crowd of family that has multiplied over the years. Beth is so glad that Will and Grant have brought Sara and Molly. She couldn't have enjoyed her company if she had to do all the work that they have done, just getting everyone fed.

Multiple times today, Beth has had to stop Chilly from putting Samuel on his six foot eight shoulders, and carrying him about, with his young nephew's head just barely missing the ceilings. "Must you be so rambunctious? You are setting a bad example for your nephew."

"What's his favorite uncle for, except to set a bad example?" Chilly responds. "At least up here, he isn't underfoot! Get it?" Beth gives him a swat to the chest which is all she can reach with her height of only five feet.

"Chilly, just behave, will you?"

"Aw, Ma. Must I?" They both smile. Chilly has always gotten away with whatever he wanted, when he uses that phrase with *that* smile.

\*\*\*

The Lawrence Gun and Sport Club has nine holes of golf, an excellent shooting range, an indoor swimming pool, and several outdoor courts for the new game of Tennis that is sweeping America. The club has several 'pros' in each sport to mentor the members. The Colonel has volunteered on the gun range regularly. It was Will who offered to use his membership to secure the banquet hall. When Carolyn learned that they had December 23rd available, she jumped up and down and kissed her older brother multiple times.

Carolyn cannot believe that was six months ago. It seemed like it was so far away, but suddenly, tomorrow is the

**116**

day. Here she is, standing at the altar of the 1st Congregational Church where her parents and all her siblings were wed. Reverend Richard Cordley is presiding over the wedding, as he had for all her family members, also. She did wear her teal gown and is smiling with tears in her eyes as they go over all the choreography of the ceremony.

Samuel will be ring bearer, and a friend of the family's four-year-old daughter will be the flower girl. Neither little one seemed to comprehend their part in the procession down the aisle, until Uncle Chilly took over. First, he carried Samuel on his shoulders, then he walked him slowly.

Joanna was a different story. She watched Samuel have the fun of the ride, but was hesitant to go so high up. She was wearing a dress so Chilly said, "Joanna, I think I will hold you differently and not so high. Do you want to ride up and down the aisle, too?" She hesitantly nodded yes, so he bent down, put his arms around the lower section of her dress and hoisted her up. She was still in standing position as he held her, and her head was just a little above his. With a very wide smile, she pretended to throw flowers out of the empty basket she was holding. They seemed to understand what to do, now and when told to do it, by themselves, they did it perfectly, together.

After the rehearsal, they all rode to the Club where they were met by their grandparents Clyde and Marilyn. Ezra arrived at the same time as Richard, which was a little strained. They had a private room that fit their party of twenty-one people perfectly.

After the wonderful meal of Chicken Marsala, they can hear music from the bar area. Carolyn looks to Grant, then to everyone else. "Anybody want to go dancing?"

Several of the couples nodded yes. Will says, "You know I promised my Julia to dance every time there is music playing."

Beth and Julia say at the same time. "And you've been so good at keeping your promises!" Every one laughs.

Grant is the first to stand. "Shall we, my dear?" When she takes his hand, he leans into her. "Let me hold you here all night if I cannot hold you at home all night."

Carolyn blushes. "Only until eleven o'clock. Then I will be off toward home like Cinderella from the ball, but earlier.

**117**

Remember, you do not see the bride or her dress on the wedding day until she comes down the aisle."

Grant looks to Will. "Have you ever met anyone so superstitious?"

"I didn't like it either, Grant, when Julia slept at Grandmother's the night before our wedding. I laid awake all night thinking about seeing her again. It was one of the longest nights I have ever had. Come my dear, let's dance." He stands and holds out his hand for his bride of three years. She gives him the smile that melts his heart and takes his hand.

Marilyn offers, "Why don't we take the little ones to the Plantation House and get them to lay down. You young ones can stay out, for as long as you like."

So, Joanna and Samuel leave with Marilyn, Mary and Clyde. Reverend Cordley bids them a good-night, also.

Beth and William, stay dancing for an hour, but since it is still early, they leave alone. The other couples dance for the rest of the evening, but Carolyn keeps close watch on the mantle clock above the bar. When it is coming close to eleven, she reminds Grant that she is going to leave. "You can't leave so soon. I forbid it, and you promised to obey."

"Not about this."

Joanna's parents, Andrew and Patricia offer to take the bride home, so they can pick up their little girl and still get a good night's sleep.

Carolyn has gotten her wrap, but is now hesitant about leaving. "Now that the moment has arrived, I don't want to leave you, either." She puts her head on his shoulder. She lifts it slightly. "I must be strong. Give us a good kiss good-night, and I will be on my way. Tomorrow will not get here soon enough."

Grant looks at her, sadly. "This is all nonsense, wife. There is no reason for us to part for the night.

This strengthens her resolve. "No, there is every reason for it. We are talking about our whole future together. And I will ensure it is a long and happy one. Starting with your not seeing me on the wedding day until I walk down the aisle."

She gives him a peck on the cheek, puts her wrap over her shoulders and without waiting for his reply, she walks out of the bar into Andrew's waiting carriage. He follows her out, and calls to her, "I am blowing you a kiss, Carolyn." He puts his hand to his face kisses it and pretends to throw it to her.

She leans out of the carriage, and pretends to snatch it out of the air. She places it on her cheek and yells "Kisses" back to him as the carriage starts its journey and is moving too fast for her to do anything more.

The Colonel is right behind him. "Come, groom, let me buy you a drink before the brisk ride home. Julia is tiring, so we will be leaving shortly."

They walk back in together, and Grant's sister approaches him. "This is for the best, brother. This night will go by fast. I hardly remember my last night's vigil. But I do remember the nights that followed! Oh, but you've had that pleasure. The benefits of eloping!" She blushes. "I think I have had one wine too many. Forgive my boldness."

"Nothing to forgive, sister. That was that very benefit that made us elope. We could not wait to be in each other's arms. But now I must spend a long night alone. Colonel, you offered me a drink. I will take you up on that."

# TWENTY-THREE

## Saturday, December 23rd, 1882 in Lawrence

Carolyn sighs and opens her eyes. She is momentarily disappointed that her Grant isn't next to her. Then, she remembers that today is the Eve of Christmas Eve – her wedding day!!!

She yawns, stretches and smiles. "This is my wedding day!!" She yells out loud.

Chilly has the room next to her. "We know!! You aren't walking down the aisle until eleven! Let us sleep, PLEASE!

Carolyn jumps out of bed, and goes to the wall between them and pounds on it. "This is my wedding day, and if I am up - Everyone is up!!"

She throws on her dressing gown, and runs out of the bedroom. "Everyone, get up! It is my wedding day!!"

Chilly sticks his head out of the room. "If you don't let me sleep, I swear I will go get Grant and let him see you! Now be quiet!"

She goes to him. "Sorry, little brother. But how can you sleep on a day like today. Aren't you excited?"

"Not in the slightest. You are excited enough for all of us. Just keep it down." He closes his door, at the same time their parents' door opens.

"Carolyn, this is still really early. Didn't you get in rather late, last night?"

"No, I was in bed before midnight. Fast asleep the moment my head hit the pillow. I thought I would toss and turn with nerves all night, but I didn't. Eloping was the best thing I could have done. I would recommend it to everyone! I am going to put on the coffee. Are you coming, Mother?" She takes Beth's hand.

"Do I have a choice? You are too much, my girl."

\*\*\*

With everyone breakfasted by eight-thirty, Beth goes to Carolyn's room to assist the bride with getting ready. "The kitchen is cleaned up. We can go put some tendrils in your hair with the hot iron on the stove."

"Oh, yes, please. Put them all around my face. Then I will put the rest in an up-do. You could hot iron the top. That will look so romantic. They curl and pin every hair in place. Carolyn has so much wavy hair that once curled, the volume doubles. Carolyn goes back into the bedroom. Her mother goes into her room for the dress. Beth calls to Marjorie. "Margie, can you come help with the wedding dress?"

Katherine follows Margie into the bedroom. "I'd like to help. This is the most beautiful dress!"

It takes the three of them to get her into the dress, and button it up. Beth goes back to her bedroom to get the veil. Carolyn is sitting at her dressing table looking in the mirror when her mother comes into the room. She stands behind her, and holds up the crown of the veil. "I don't know where you want this attached."

Carolyn reaches for it, and looks back in the mirror. "It will go perfectly, this way." She places it at the highpoint of the front 'puff,' as she calls it. The open area right behind the crown is where they pinned the tiny curls. Carolyn deftly unpins all the curls, and she unravels them so they hang down the outside of the back of the veil. She is doing this by feel, but when she has them all unpinned she takes a hand mirror, and turns to look at her work. "See Mother, this is perfect!"

"Just perfect!" Beth, Marjorie and Katherine all say at the same time.

"I will leave the little ones pinned around my face until we get to the Church. I have the additional veil that will attach to the front of the crown for the beginning of the ceremony so that my groom does not see my face yet my top curls will be showing before and after. I just need to put a little rouge on my cheeks and I am ready to be wed. It is your turn to get dressed. Go on, everyone. Go get ready."

There is a knock on the door. It is Julia, who will be a bridesmaid, as will Lizzie. Marjorie will be the Maid of Honor. Carolyn came very close to choosing Julia as Matron of Honor. Julia has been as close as any sister to her and Marjorie, but her sister Marjorie has always been her closest friend in the world.

All the bridesmaid dresses are in Beth's room, too. Julia says, "Come girls; we need to dress, it is getting late! Not that we will ever be as beautiful as the bride." Carolyn stands to hug her sister-in-law twice over.

Beth interrupts, "Stay here and relax, Carolyn. We don't want you to do too much. No sign of your courses?"

"No Momma. I hope there will be no sign of that today, or any day."

"I have prayed for this, since this is your wish."

"At first I was upset, but then I thought of what a miracle it will be for a baby to grow in my womb from the love Grant and I share. What could be better?"

"You are asking the wrong woman. Don't forget, I delivered eight little ones."

"Yes, I remember. Grant and I will stop at four, if the good Lord wills that we reach that number. Go, Mother, get dressed for my wedding. I will just sit here, and bide my time until we are all ready to leave."

\*\*\*

After Julia left to go the Plantation House to dress, Grant and Will, who are already properly attired, have a lively game of chess. Before they know it, they are late for leaving. Grant says, "If Carolyn sees that I am not in the church's windowless groom's room when she gets there, she will not get out of the carriage. AND she will be mad enough to kill."

"I will tell her to blame me for making you late." The Colonel says as he is hitching the horses to the buggy.

"IT IS *YOUR* FAULT! Just one quick game, you said. I haven't played in so long, you said. It will calm your nerves, you said. If she doesn't forgive me, I won't forgive you, Brother!" Grant is raving like a madman, as Will is making the horse run at full gallop.

They arrive at the church, in just a few minutes. There are lots of buckboards in the lot, but no sign of the bride's rented carriage. Grant breathes a sigh of relief. "That was too close. I am still telling your sister what you did. Best man, my derrière!" He gives a small punch to Will's shoulder.

"Stop fooling around, and get into that room. I think

this is them coming!!" Will yells.

Grant hops down from the buggy and hears a rip from the seat of his pants. "Great! Now my pants are torn! There is no time for this. See if you can find someone with a needle and thread. I will wait in the groom's room." He hurries off.

Will looks at his pocket watch. They only have fifteen minutes until the bride is supposed to walk down the aisle. Will, suddenly, imagines that Grant is waiting for Carolyn at the altar in his shirt, and tails, but no pants! He jumps down, himself, and goes into the church. Luckily, Grandmother Marilyn is there. "Grandmother, do you have a needle and thread? Grant has ripped his pants."

Mary is next to her mother in the front seat. "Oh, my goodness, Steven did the same thing, remember Mother? This is a wonderful sign. This couple will have a blessed marriage."

"Of course I remember. That is why I have several thread colors in my bag. If it isn't the bride with a rip, it's the groom." She stands up, goes to the vestibule and knocks on the groom's room door. "Grant, it's Grandmother. Hand out your pants. I have a needle and thread, and I can sew it for you, if you hurry."

The door opens, and just an arm comes out with a pair of pants draped across them. "The rip isn't as bad as I thought, but it is in a very conspicuous spot. First, I am late, now this! So much for Carolyn's avoiding bad luck today."

"Carolyn is trying to avoid a bad marriage! That is what the superstition is about. Relax, this will only take a moment. The bride isn't here yet, so the ceremony being late will not be your fault." She is quiet for the few moments it takes to sew the twelve stitches needed to stop Grant's undergarments from showing. She breaks off the thread with her teeth, then says. "There Grandson, that should do it." She hands him back the pants. "Now, I am going back to my seat. Good luck." Without waiting for an answer, she is off back to her spot.

The carriage carrying the bride arrives at five minutes to eleven. Will meets the carriage, and escorts his wife and sisters to the bride's room, while Chilly takes his mother to her seat.

Carolyn asks, as she is rushing to the room, "Is Grant is tucked away – safe and secure?"

"Of course. I know my job, and I have executed my

duties to the best of my abilities." He winks at her, and she kisses his cheek before entering the room. Once all the women are in the room with the door closed, the Colonel goes to tell the groom to wait at the altar.

Once he is in place, the bride's father knocks on the bride's door. "Is everyone ready? He asks.

Carolyn opens the door. His one and only red-headed beauty smiles. "I was ready two weeks ago." Everyone lines up in the foyer with the doors to the church closed. William Sr. opens the doors, and the music starts.

Joanna and Samuel start their walk down the aisle. Joanna is smiling, but Samuel looks terrified with all the strangers watching. He starts to run. Joanna reaches for him and grabs him by his coat. "We have to walk slow, remember?" Samuel doesn't answer, but stays in step with her. He is wearing a scared looking smile.

Lizzie starts her decent down the aisle on the arm of her brother and business partner Joseph. When they get to the end, they part, and go to separate sides of the altar. They are followed by Julia and Chilly, arm in arm. Then comes Marjorie on the arm of the Colonel. After they part ways at the altar, Mendolssohn's Wedding March begins. Grant is anxiously waiting for her.

William holds out his arm for Carolyn, and they begin their slow walk. Carolyn's veil is now covering her face. There are oohs and aahs, as they pass. It feels to Carolyn, as if they walk four hundred feet instead of forty. When they get to the altar, William lifts the veil to kiss his daughter, then takes the hand of Grant, and puts Carolyn's hand in it. He steps back and sits beside his crying wife.

Carolyn is breathtaking. The dress is form fitting enough to accentuate her full figure, but everything is lace over satin and very modest. Grant is smiling so hard, and has tears in his eyes. She leans into him. "Happy tears," she says as one of her own escapes.

Reverend Cordley begins. "Dearly Beloved, we are gathered here today to join this man and this woman in Holy Matrimony."

As with every bride and groom, they hear just bits and pieces of the ceremony until it is their turn to say the vows.

They can miraculously hear again, when the Reverend says "You may kiss the bride." When they are done with their kiss the Reverend adds. "Ladies and Gentlemen, may I introduce Mr. and Mrs. Grant Johnson."

The couple turn and walk down the aisle to the rear of the church. Their wedding party follows them, then the family, and finally their friends. Because the weather outside is very cold again today, the reception line is in the crowded foyer. Once everyone congratulates them, they all head to the Lawrence Gun and Sport Club for the wedding luncheon. Before the wedding party leaves, they go back into the church for several photos. Pictures taken at weddings is becoming all the rage these days, and Carolyn is the first one in Lawrence to do it.

\*\*\*

Once at the banquet hall, more photos are taken. The room is decorated in pink and teal streamers and table cloths. The wedding party forms a reception line to greet all the guests. Because of the standing of Beth and William in the community, as well as the Colonel's community service, there are five hundred guests invited. Grant hardly knows anyone, but he doesn't care. Grant thinks Carolyn is the most beautiful woman in the world and he wants to show her off. She is HIS, and now everyone knows it.

It takes an hour of standing in line while the guests enjoy appetizers and a string quartet. The luncheon consists of four courses. Salad, choice of two soups – tomato bisque or cheesy potato, choice of two entrees – Steak Diane or peach glazed pork chops. Desert is cherries jubilee and almond ice cream and later, of course – almond flavored wedding cake with strawberry filling. Everyone is amazed at the grandeur of it all.

The wedding party all sit at a long table facing the room. The happy couple are in the center. Several times throughout the meal, people would clink their wine glasses with their spoons for the bride and groom to kiss. It's an old custom that started long ago when it was thought the clinking sound would drive the devil away, making it safe for the bride and groom to kiss.

After everyone has eaten, a band sets up for dancing. As they set up, the happy couple disappear and a garden archway is set up near the doorway. The band plays a small soft song then the leader of the band says. "Ladies and Gentlemen. It is my pleasure to announce the new Mr. and Mrs. Grant Johnson." They walk in under the archway, and wait a moment while the photographer takes another picture. Then they approach the center of the room. The guest tables are all moved to make room for dancing. When in the center of the dance floor, Grant takes his most beautiful Carolyn in his arms. As the music begins to play, the world around them disappears as they stare into each other's eyes.

Soon, the wedding party takes to the floor. The Colonel exchanges Marjorie for his Julia. Others begin to join them, and after a while, there is hardly any room for other dancers. Grant and his Carolyn don't even notice.

# TWENTY-FOUR

## Sunday, December 24th, 1882 in Lawrence

The bride and groom spend the night in the bridal suite of the Lawrence Hotel. The reservation was booked months in advance. They each had their bags in the buggies so that they can go straight there when the reception was over. They had a room-service champagne dinner. Then had another bottle brought up an hour later.

Since Grant had borrowed the Colonel's buggy for the get-a-way, the Colonel rode in the rented bridal carriage back to the Plantation. They were the last to leave but still arrived home a little before nine. Sara and Molly had a light supper waiting and everyone talked about the wonderful event that their little sister orchestrated.

Today, being Christmas Eve, Joseph and Will are taking Samuel to pick out a Christmas tree. They brought the old sled that the family used when they were all young to carry Samuel and eventually the tree.

The Colonel had purchased this new parcel of land to the west of their original holdings because it was loaded with natural conifer pine trees. At some point in the future, the Colonel would like to offer these trees to the public. As they get cut down, he will plant a new one to replace it.

With saw in hand, the Colonel is leading the way with Joseph pulling Samuel on the sled. "Samuel, I want you to look out for a tree taller than me, but with no bare spots. Let me know when you see one."

"Not tall like Daddy?" He asks. Joseph is barely six feet tall.

"No, we don't want a puny tree. We want a real big one!" The Colonel laughs. Joseph is the only one of the Lewis boys that took after Beth's shorter side of the family. He also is smaller boned than Ian, Will or Chilly.

"That's cruel, little brother!"

"Daddy? Why do you call my uncles 'little brother'? They are both soooo big."

"I am not talking about their height. I am referring to

**127**

the fact that they are younger than me."

"Oh, like Connie is younger?"

"Yes, you will be the oldest and every other brother or sister will be your 'little' brother or sister no matter how tall they get."

"That's funny! I want to be the tallest, as big as my Uncles."

"So did I, Samuel, but for me it just wasn't meant to be. You have a good chance. Gram Beth says you are as big as Chilly was, when he was your age."

"Chilly was my age?"

The brothers laugh. Joseph says, "Samuel, we were all your age at one point. Even Great Grandfather Clyde was your age."

"You are telling me a fib. I am telling Momma."

The Colonel stops walking. "Samuel, what do you think of this tree? It's very tall, but not too wide on the bottom. No bare spots." He says as he walks around it a second time. "I think this is the one. What do you think, big Brother? Samuel?" They both agree.

Soon, the tree is on the sled and Samuel is on the Colonel's shoulders, as they head back to the Plantation House. They get to the house and go inside, Samuel runs to Clyde, and climbs on his lap.

"Grampa Clyde, were you little like me, once?"

Clyde laughs at the question. "I was! It was a long, long time ago. I am seventy-seven years old. If I had a candle on the cake for each year since I was born, I'd burn the house down." He chuckled. "Why do you ask?"

"Daddy told me you were little like me, but I thought he was fibbing!" Then he says very seriously. "How did you get so old?"

Clyde starts to laugh. He laughs so hard that his belly shakes Samuel off his lap. The Colonel and Joseph are laughing too, and each time they slow down, they start all over again.

Samuel is just looking at them all. When his mother comes into the room, he runs to her. "Mommy, I made a funny. They laugh too hard at me!"

"No, honey. No one is laughing at you. But, you did

make a funny!" His father tries to explain.

Clyde calls to him. "Samuel, you made a good funny! Come here and let Grandpa give you a kiss for making me laugh so much. Laughter is good for you and you are good at helping us laugh, little one." Samuel comes back to his oversized Great Grandpa, and climbs back in the little area that remains of his lap. "You are my favorite little boy. Do you know that?" He gives another chuckle. He bends over and kisses his forehead. "I wish that you can stay here forever." He looks to Katherine. "Do you think you can send him here to spend the summers? Marilyn and Beth will spoil him to death. And his Uncle Chilly will teach him all kinds of slimy, dirty fun things that boys should do as a youngin'."

"That would be nice for him. Maybe when he is old enough for school, he can come for a few weeks each summer, and learn what it is like to work a farm." Joseph adds, "and another helping hand around here would be appreciated, I am sure. What do you think, Katherine?"

"Not until he is school-age, but yes. It will do a boy good to learn the hard work of the family farm business."

\*\*\*

At four o'clock, the tree is still being decorated by the whole family. Grant and Carolyn come back for the festivities and Christmas Eve dinner. They have come with arms loaded with packages. "Merry Christmas, everyone." Carolyn shouts as she enters the house. She looks to Samuel. "We saw Santa Claus, and he said that he will be here tonight - if you go to sleep on time."

"Santa Claus? You saw him? I want to see him!"
He is still on Clyde's lap. "You look like Santa with your big belly and your white beard. You just need a red suit."

"I never thought about that. I will get one next year and play Santa!"

Marilyn walks into the room from the kitchen. "As much as you love little ones, you would make the best Santa. You are so good with them." She goes over and pinches his face. "Samuel, you are sure smart. Would you like Grampa Clyde to pretend to be Santa?"

129

"Yes!!! Grampa Santa! Grampa Santa! More presents!!"

Clyde starts laughing again. "Not more presents, little one. There is still only one Santa, I would just pretend to be Santa at Christmas parties and such. I think."

\*\*\*

Christmas Eve dinner was a long, loud affair. The siblings shared nonstop childhood stories. Mary Johnson moved to Lawrence in 1866, so Grant and Julia were always involved in the Lewis family doings. It allows them to share lots of memories. Grant is four years younger than Joseph and four years older than Will. This made him an 'in-between-er' who didn't play much with any of the Lewis boys, but they were still family at all the Holidays, parties and social events.

Once again, Beth is standing back just watching the crowd. She looks to her oldest living child. "Joseph, did you get enough to eat?" How about you, Katherine? You are too skinny after just giving birth. You need to get some meat on your bones."

The Colonel interrupts, "My Julia needs a second helping!"

"Will, I couldn't eat another bite. You are just saying that so that you can pick from 'my' plate, as usual. I swear, he and Chilly are bottomless pits."

Beth just laughs and says, "Thank God. A healthy appetite is such a blessing!"

Her husband behind her says, "Yes, but someday, those blessings will turn into pounds, like mine did. Beware!!"

# TWENTY-FIVE

## Tuesday, December 26ᵗʰ, 1882 in Lawrence

Yesterday, Christmas Day, started with eight o'clock Christmas Service at the First Congregational Church. Reverend Cordley kept his sermons short, so that the school children could present a nativity play. The crowd loved it. Some of the children playing the animals were a little confused on where to go and what to do, which made it even more adorable.

After service, everyone returned to the Plantation House and presents were opened and a large breakfast was served. Holidays like this traditionally have only two meals, both large ones. Once again, Carolyn went to the pianoforte and everyone got involved with singing all the old Christmas Carols and the one new one. It was the best Christmas, ever!

Unfortunately, all good things must come to an end. Earlier this morning, Lizzie and Ezra, and Joseph and his family left on the first train for Wichita.

Carolyn and Grant will be heading back to Lawrence, tomorrow. Carolyn has her room in complete disarray. Beth complains, "I don't know why you can't stay. There is the New Year's dance next weekend, and lots to do before that."

"Mother, I need to MOVE into my husband's home. Grant ordered two steamer trunks for me last week and they will be delivered today. I need to go through all my clothing and pack. There are all the lovely things in my hope chest, also."

Grant comes into Carolyn's room as she and her mother are talking. "Carolyn, I had an idea. Why don't we host a small dinner reception on Sunday to announce our marriage? Just a few people, my step-family and a few of my close friends. Mother said she would take the train home to be there for it. Beth, you and William are invited to join her."

"Did you say step-family?" Carolyn is shocked.

"Yes, I want to send telegrams to Aunt Gloria, Aunt Helen and especially Auntie June telling them that I want them to meet my new bride. You know the curiosity of older ladies?

They will kill to be there to meet you."

"Is this part of your plan to stop your Uncle Ben?"

"It could be.  We hope so."

"We?"

"Oh, yes.  The Colonel and Julia are coming out with Mother, also."

"Grant, I do not like how mysterious you are being.  You had me so worried when you and my brothers went on that road trip."

"I'll give you more details on the road.  I promise.  Well, Beth, you won't have to be separated from Carolyn, but for a few days, and you can help get her settled in.  Do you like the idea?"

Carolyn has a huge smile on. "Momma, that will be so nice!  You haven't been to the Farmhouse since Will was a newlywed and Julia took sick.  This would be a great trip for you."

Beth looks torn. "I don't know.  Marjorie has a date with two different suiters on Sunday.  I want to be here for her.  Let me talk to your father and sleep on it."

# TWENTY-SIX

## Friday, December 29th, 1882 in EL Dorado

Carolyn and Grant made excellent time on the road with all of Carolyn's belongings. She had three loaded steamer trunks plus her hope chest. In her hope chest is her maternal grandmother's - her namesake's china service for 12. Every piece is carefully wrapped and has been stored in the chest since her passing in 1859. Her mother was pregnant with Will and her Grandmother was convinced that he would be a girl. She made her pregnant daughter swear that if she passed, this set would go to her namesake, even though Beth had two girls before she named her fourth daughter Carolyn. It was after her naming that Beth remembered the china set and the promise.

The couple arrived at the Farmhouse late in the night and Annabelle and Clarence were very efficient at moving all of Carolyn's things in and unpacking them. They also brought in help to get everything 'spit spot' clean as Annabelle likes to say. Carolyn had purchased new bedding for all the bedrooms, and she and Annabelle plan to spend the rest of the day changing out all the linens

Tomorrow, Mary, Julia and Will are coming in by train. Clarence will be getting them. Carolyn has been working with Annie on her mother's recipes for the dinner reception. Beth will not be attending, which saddened Carolyn and made her nervous about hosting her first dinner without her help.

Each of the guests who were telegrammed responded that they are very happy to attend. There will be twenty-one for the sit-down dinner. Carolyn has met fewer than half of them, but she feels like she knows most of them through Grant's talking about them over the years.

Grant comes into the Farmhouse calling for her. "Car-O-lyn, come quickly, where are you? Car-O-lyn?"

Carolyn lets go of her end of the sheet she was holding. She looks to Annabelle. "What's is going on?" She leaves the bedroom and walks to the railing of the staircase and calls down. "I am upstairs, Grant. What is wrong?"

It's Joan of Arc! She is giving birth to your wedding

**133**

present! Come meet your new foal! Hurry!"

Carolyn flies down the stairs and grabs her wrap from the coat tree by the door. "It's about time! You thought she was going to deliver a month ago. This is so exciting." Grant helps her with the coat, takes her hand and they run down to the stable. "Is Clarence with her?" As they enter the stable they hear the horse crying out. "Oh, she is in pain, Grant. Will she be all right?"

"I have never seen a foal being born without the mother crying like that. It is the only sound they make like it, their whole life. That is how I knew it was time."

They get to her stall, and Clarence is bringing more hay to soak up the mess that is soon to come. Joan of Arc is standing, legs far apart, and her tail is up and bent. You can tell she is straining. Grant says to the horse, "You waited for us, didn't you? I hoped you would, my beautiful girl." He is stroking her head, and she is calming down. "Lay down girl, it will be easier on you."

Joan of Arc starts walking around in small circles, and the amniotic sac is starting to protrude out. As she tightens the circle walk, she starts to leak, then floods, and she go down at the same time. "Good girl, your water broke. That will help." Grant says reassuringly.

As she lays down, more sac comes out and Grant reaches over and pulls on it to reveal two legs just barely sticking out. Joan is panting and moving around. She even rolls on her back for a moment. She suddenly stands back up and the legs go back in. "Come on girl, it's okay." He says as he pets her hip area.

"Grant, how many times have you been through this?" Carolyn asks. "I am shocked at how comfortable you are with this."

"I used to help the stable man, before I moved to Lawrence. My mother was afraid that the horse would kick me, but the mares always knew that I was trying to help. Joan's mother was the last foal born before I moved. I was just eleven, but Hershel let me pull the foal out. I told you that I am not squeamish when it comes to womanly issues." He has his hands on the foal's legs as Joan decides to lay back down, she almost takes him with her. Before she is fully down, Grant

**134**

yanks hard and the babe is born. He reaches over to remove the sac from around the nostrils. "Oh, look at you, a little cutie like your mother." He pulls the sac away from most of its body and announces, "Carolyn, you have a new filly. There, there, little one, stay down till I get you all cleaned up." The filly has a mind of her own, and before he has the sac away from her legs, she brings her legs under her and stands. "This filly is going to be a winner. Look how strong she is just after birth!"

Even though he is standing there with his hands slimy and full of blood, Carolyn goes to him to hug and kiss him. He forgets about his hands, and hugs and kisses her back. "You are getting all messy!" He says when he comes to his senses.

"I don't care. This is the best present, ever! Look at her. Her ears are all back, and she is still slimy, and hay is sticking to her everywhere, but I have never seen anything more beautiful!" She says with tears in her eyes. "And she is mine, all mine!"

"You might have to fight Joan for her for a little while, but yes, she is all yours. I knew that you'd be happy with this. I knew that this would be the perfect wedding gift!"

"Yes, Grant. You gave me the perfect gift, and I hope to match it in nine months!" She blushes in front of Clarence, who is cleaning up the stall. She leans in and whispers. "We are still on track for that event by the way." She winks at him.

"I know, Darling. I couldn't be happier. I love you so much, Carolyn."

"And I, you."

"Have you thought of a name for your little girl?"

"Not quite yet. I am going to have to ponder this for a while. I have a few ideas in mind, though."

# TWENTY-SEVEN

## Saturday, December 30th, 1882 in EL Dorado

Will, his Julia, and Mary are on the ten o'clock train. Clarence took Carolyn to pick them up. Carolyn is hoping that her mother changed her mind, and will surprise her by being on the train. Will is the first one down, and he helps his mother-in-law then his wife. He lifts Julia high into the air. "You still need to gain some weight, my love. Please ask for seconds at all meals until you build yourself up." He puts her down.

"You would have me fat, my love?" She smiles at him. "If I started eating like that, when will it stop?"

They turn to face Carolyn. "You two are the perfect example for me. Guess what? Joan of Arc had her filly last night. She stood up while the sac was still on half of her body. True race horse stamina. Not to mention that she is so beautiful."

Julia grabs her arm and pulls her forward. "What still needs to be done for the dinner party? Who is invited and who has responded? What are we serving?"

Mary rushes forward and takes Carolyn's other arm. "Yes, yes, tell us all."

Clarence and the Colonel retrieve the luggage while the ladies go to the buggy. The Colonel looks to Clarence. "Has everything been set up, as per my wire?"

"Yes, sir, Colonel. Master Grant got it all taken care of. Don't worry about that none." Clarence says with a smile.

Two hours later, the women are in the kitchen making, baking and stirring an overabundance of food. Some of it is for today, but most of it is for tomorrow. Carolyn is not sure which dish will turn out like her mother's, so she is rehearsing each recipe.

Carolyn asks Mary and Julia for some extra information about her invited guests. Mary starts. "Larkin Bailey will be sworn in as our new sheriff on January 2nd. Grant was a great supporter, and was his best man when he was wed to Monica. She has a four-month-old, so be prepared for endless baby stories. You know new mothers. Her Larkin, Jr. will be the next president of the United States. Well, at least in her eyes. Then there are the Curtises. Miles and Sara. He is a lawyer, and she went to primary school with Julia. Then there are the Walkers. Chandler and Jenna. He went to school with Grant, and they also own race horses. Grant also invited Benjamin Ford. He is Antonia's nephew, and the namesake of Ben Johnson. He is a widower, and was always very nice to me. Girls, I am feeling very tired. I am going upstairs to rest before dinner. Just call me."

"Yes, of course, Mother. Thank you for all your help. Do you want help up the stairs?"

"No, my dear. Stay and work on your party planning." She kisses Carolyn and leaves the room for her nap.

Carolyn turns to Julia. "I am so nervous. I hope I can keep them all straight." She looks around at all the food. "I am also starving. How could I not be? Surrounded by all this food?" She laughs. "Or am I eating for two?"

Julia blushes. "I was afraid to ask. Still no sign of your monthly, then?"

Carolyn shakes her head. "My friend has taken a leave of absence. So far so good."

Julia says, "I hope it is so. I wouldn't wish my trouble on my worst enemy. I conceive easily enough, but I never seem to be able to get past the third month."

Carolyn says, "I feel so bad about that. Will you be Godmother to my babe? Whenever I have a babe?"

"I will, if you are Godmother to mine?"

"Deal!" Carolyn holds out her hand for Julia to shake it. Then she pulls her into a hug. "You know that I could not love you more if you were my sister by blood instead of marriage."

"I feel the same way. And to see you so happy with Grant. It is so perfect. Now, let me tell you my version of some of the guests."

\*\*\*

At two in the afternoon, there is a delivery. Grant tells Julia to keep Carolyn busy in the kitchen because he wants to surprise her after it is all set up. Carolyn almost refuses to leave the room. She has arranged the parlor perfectly, and now he is going to move everything for whatever he has bought.

Julia coaxes her. "Carolyn, I am sure that it will be fine. Come on, let Grant be the Master of the house and surprise you with something."

Carolyn was about to object. Grant walks up to her. "Love, honor and OBEY, woman. Just this once, please?" He raises her left hand and brushes it with his lips. "Please?" He says again.

"Fine, since you put it that way." She removes her hand from his, and slaps his shoulder. "I'd better like it or you are going to be sorry."

"I am taking a calculated risk. I know. Now get!"

Julia leads her out of the parlor, and back in the kitchen. "You too are great sparing partners. So fun to watch. Will and I never talk to each other that way. You are so free to say what you think. You have so much confidence in yourself. Where does it come from?"

"Have you met my mother?"

"I know, but she and Father do not spare. They act more as one mind in two bodies."

"That's true, but . . . I feel that they did in the beginning of their union.

They are in the kitchen for a half an hour. Carolyn looks at Julia, "What could be taking so long? This is ridiculous. I am going out there." She gets up from the table, and heads to the doorway, just as Grant walks through it. "Oh, thank goodness. I was just going to sneak a peek. Is it ready?"

Okay, Carolyn. I know it was hard for you to wait. Can you close your eyes? I will lead you out."

"Grant, this is too much, isn't it?" She says as he leads her out. His hands are over her eyes just in case she tries to peak. "I think this is so silly, keeping my eyes closed. What have you done?" They are finally at the entranceway to the parlor. He removes his hands, and she opens her eyes. "Really, Grant? What is it?"

From behind her, she hears Julia gasp. This makes Carolyn turn around. "What?"

Julia points, "Look – oh my goodness. What a great surprise!"

Carolyn turns back to look where Julia is pointing. In the back of the parlor is a shiny baby grand piano. Not a little pianoforte like she had in EL Dorado, but a full-size piano. "Grant, what did you do? This is mine? All mine? Can we afford this? After the expense of the wedding, the forged letter, and the trip to Wichita? How rich are we or is this the end of it?" She is talking a mile a minute as she practically runs to the new piano. "I am sure it needs to be tuned. No piano comes sounding good." She plays a few notes. "It isn't bad."

"The tuner is on his way. I wanted you to see it before it gets tuned. You would have heard the notes everywhere, even in this large house."

"Grant, you are so good to me! How do I deserve someone so generous? My own racehorse and my own piano! My own loving husband! Kiss me, you fool."

He rushes to her. "Your wish is my command." His lips are on hers, and her arms are immediately around his neck. She leans in to press herself against him. She suddenly breaks away. "What is it?"

"That hurt." She says folding her arms across her bosom. "That is so odd."

A small voice speaks from behind Grant. They forgot Julia was in the room. "Not if you are with child. My top gets very sensitive. It's the first sign for me."

Carolyn smiles. "I can't wait to find out with certainty. I am not very patient."

"We know." Grant and his little sister say at the same time. Then everyone laughs.

Mary comes into the parlor. "A white piano? When did that get here? Was it here all day, and I missed it? I must be getting old to have missed a whole piano."

"Oh, Mother Mary. My husband just had it delivered. Aren't my piano and my Grant, grand?"

# TWENTY-EIGHT

## Sunday, December 31ˢᵗ, 1882 in EL Dorado

The morning of the Dinner Reception was very busy. All the cooking the day before was a rehearsal for today. Last night, Carolyn finally decided the menu. Annabelle has her orders. She starts baking the first thing in the morning. Fresh bread baking is the smell that wakes Carolyn with a sigh and a smile. "I hope that is for breakfast. I am starving!" Grant is asleep next to her. This is the first time since they have been married that she woke before him.

"What? Carolyn, did you say something?" He opens his eyes. "Boy, that bread smells good. I am starving." He smiles. "Sorry, my stomach is grumbling."

"What are we waiting for? Let's get downstairs." She is out of the bed, and in her gown before Grant can finish rubbing the sleep from his eyes. "Slow poke, get up! We have lots to do, and I cannot do it with my stomach this empty. I feel like I swallowed a bucket of holes. Is that what yours feels like?"

"As with everything else, we are a perfect match." He gets up and puts on his dressing gown. Carolyn doesn't wait. She is out the door, and down the stairs before he has the time to tie his belt.

\*\*\*

The telegrams read: The honor of your presence is requested to meet my new bride, the former Carolyn Lewis of Lawrence, for an early Dinner Reception at 6 p.m. at the Johnson Farmhouse. Please R.S.V.P. at your earliest convenience. Grant Johnson, owner of Johnson Family Farms.

Lizzie and Ezra are the first to arrive. They came on the stagecoach, and will be leaving Monday night. Clarence met them in town, and brought them to the Farmhouse. Carolyn is wearing a ball gown with a green scalloped bodice and a black skirted bottom. She has her hair perfectly curled in a large chignon. Julia is wearing the peach color dress that was a present from the happy couple. The Colonel is in his tails as is Grant. Mary comes down in a beautiful dark green gown.

The next to arrive is EL Dorado's soon-to-be sheriff Larkin Bailey, Sr., and his wife Monica. Grant gives Larkin a big hug. Larkin says, "There is our best man! How did you not invite us to Lawrence? We would have loved to have been there for the ceremony."

Grant leans in to explain. "Sorry, Larkin. It was a circus. Five hundred people at the reception. With all of Lawrence attending, there was little room for my EL Dorado friends and family. This intimate setting is more to my style. Come on in and meet my wife."

Aunt Gloria and Uncle Elmer came next. She had a beautifully wrapped present for the young bride. "Darling, welcome to the family. Elmer, look at her. She is the definition of charm and loveliness."

Elmer being a man of few words says, "How do?"

Uncle George and his wife Aunt Helen came next. Helen was sweet as Aunt Gloria. "Carolyn, I am so happy to meet you." Uncle George grunts with a smile on his face.

Miles Curtis and his wife Sara come with Reverend Scott. Sara is new with child and glowing. "Carolyn, it is good to finally meet you. Your time in EL Dorado has been so short with each visit, with most of your courting being in Lawrence." She gives Carolyn a kiss on the cheek. "I feel we are going to be life-long friends. Don't you?"

Chandler and Jenna Walker arrive. "Where is the new bride? Did Joan of Arc foal yet?" Chandler comes in, his usual talkative self.

Jenna elbows him in the ribs. "Don't spoil it."

Carolyn counters, "I know that Grant was keeping it a secret, but he and she gave me a filly, two days ago. The little girl is a true champion. She stood with her hind legs still in the birth sac. Strong breeding shows."

"Thank you, Carolyn. It was our stud Galahad that sired her. Standing so early is a great sign." Chandler continues. "Does she have a name yet? The name is as important as the parentage in my book."

Jenna takes Carolyn's hands. "Don't rush it. Her name

will come to you, and will be perfect when it is decided. Welcome to Lawrence, and welcome to exciting sport of horseracing. Do you ride? I love the feel of the wind in my face. I have some friends who think it is barbaric that I enjoy riding. Please, do not be one of them. I so need a riding partner."

Carolyn smiles. "Well, meet your new partner, then. How soon do you want to go out? Do you like to ride in the winter?"

"Absolutely, it is very stimulating! Let's plan on Wednesday, then. Come to my stables and you can have your choice of horses."

The next doorbell ringer is an elderly gentleman. He is Grant's step-cousin, Grandmother Antonia's nephew, Benjamin Ford who shared more than the last name with his aunt. They shared the incredible light hazel eyes. When he approaches Carolyn, she is dumbfounded momentarily, seeing the resemblance to Theo and Antonia. "Cousin Ben, it is so good to meet you." She says, quickly, to cover up her unease.

Finally, the last to arrive is the blackmailer, Uncle Ben and his wife, Auntie June. Ben looks like a caged animal as he enters the house. June gives him a nervous look, but says, "Thank you, Grant for the invitation. I know that there were hard feelings when you first inherited, but I see that you have forgiven us, and put that all behind you. Now, introduce us to your bride. I hear she is quite the beauty."

They have hired waiters to serve drinks, the hors devours and the canapés. They spend twenty minutes in the parlor getting to know the bride. Aunt Gloria sees the piano and says. "What a beautiful addition! Carolyn, do you play? You must give us a taste of your talent."

"Oh, I do not think that I feel comfortable doing that tonight. I do not have any of my sheet music. Grant just presented me with it today. I would have brought my music from Lawrence, had I known, but . . ."

Will overhears her. "Nonsense Sis. Once you play something twice, your fingers have committed the piece to its memory. Don't sell yourself short."

Annabelle has come into the room and whispers something to Grant. Grant walks to an end table, picks up a

**142**

little bell and rings it. "Attention everyone, dinner is served. Please come into the dining room."

Carolyn lets out a breath of air. *Saved by the bell.* She then announces. "Everybody, there are place cards at each setting. Please find your name and take a seat." She ushers everyone into the dining room.

Reverend Scott finds himself seated between Aunt Gloria and her brother George. The Reverend is telling the story of Clarence's urgent mission to bring him to the Farmhouse for a midnight wedding. Aunt Gloria is all ears. She asks him why they needed to be wed in such a hurry with the Lawrence event all planned. The Reverend explains. "Grant said that something came up that he wasn't sure would be cleared up before he could travel to Lawrence. They wanted to be man and wife, more than any other couple I have had the pleasure to marry."

Aunt Gloria looks to her host at the head of the table and asks, "Nephew, what could have possibly come up that would cause you to miss your own wedding?"

Grant looks at Ben and smiles. "It was a small matter, but I think it is behind us, now. It turned out to be a blessing in disguise. I had telegrammed my fiancée that I will be delayed. My beautiful, but brave Carolyn came to my rescue. Well, she and her very courageous brothers. Chilly was our best man and Will gave the bride away. It was perfect. Of course, it was just a rehearsal for the real deal on the 23rd." He smiled at Carolyn. "Right my darling Wife?

"I would not have had it any other way, Husband." She smiles back and blushes.

Uncle George smiles looking from the bride and groom and stands up. "May I toast to the very happy couple?"

"Hear. Hear!" Everyone lifts their glass to join in the toast. All except Uncle Ben, that is.

All during the dinner, Uncle Ben's eyes dart from Grant to Carolyn, then to the Colonel. More than once, Auntie June leans over to him and tries to find the reason for his unease. He just waves her away. Carolyn smiles. Her imagination sees the discussion that took place at the arrival of the telegram.

June: 'Oh look, we are invited to a small wedding

**143**

dinner.'

Ben: 'We can't go.'

June: 'Why not, we have no other commitments.'

Ben: 'I don't trust Grant. Too many hard feelings.'

June: 'Well, I think he handing us an olive branch here. I want to go.'

Ben: 'Well, I don't!'

June: 'Give me a reason, why not?'

Then silence on Ben's part. Carolyn sees it all perfectly in her mind's eye, and gives a snicker.

Cornish hens and prime rib are the entrée choices. Everyone is extremely complimentary. Even with all the courses and conversation, the meal service goes quickly. Carolyn sees Aunt Gloria look at her watch, which makes her look at the mantle clock.

Will sees that, also and says, "Sis, that was the best meal, ever. Since it is still early, would you do us all a favor and play something on your new piano? Julia did bring your new music for 'Away in the Manger'. Will you, please, do us the favor and sing it for us?"

Grant stands. "I agree, you must play, darling. Let me show you off to everyone. You sing so beautifully." Several of the guests stand and urge her to play. "Please, as a favor for me?" Grant adds.

Carolyn gives in. "Julia, you have my music?" She asks, surprised.

"Yes, just the one. You sang it so brilliantly that I hoped you would sing it again for me. Let me go get it. I will be right back." As Julia excuses, herself, everyone else stands, gets a fresh glass of sherry poured, and moves back into the parlor.

Julia comes down the stairs, breathless. "Here dear. I am looking forward to this."

Carolyn takes the music from her, and sits down at the piano. She looks around the room. When she sees her husband, she calls to him, and pats the seat next to her, for him to sit. When he does so, she begins playing.

Though nerves have a hold of her, her voice is clear and pitch perfect. "Away in the Manger . . ." she begins. When she gets to the next verse, two young voices join hers. She looks

**144**

around, and little Antonia and Theo are singing.  Theo is in white pants and shirt.  Antonia has on a beautiful white dress.  Their voices are angelic.  They know the song from all the singing of it that they did on the road.  Carolyn smiles.  This was the Colonel's plan, and she played right into his hands.  When she is finished with the whole song, she turns to the audience who are speechless, but applauding.  Carolyn says, 'Thank you, everyone.  I am sure that it is as much for my accompanists as for myself."  She turns to the little ones.  "Great job, you were just perfect."  She applauding them, also.  She turns back to her guests.  "We have practiced a few other songs.  Would you like us to sing you another . . .?"

Ben does not let her finish.  He jumps up and exclaims.  "I cannot believe you are doing this.  Using innocent children this way!  That is so low of you all.  I do not have to stand for this.  June, we are leaving."  He pulls her to a stand.

"Ben, what has come over you.  What is wrong the children singing?  Why are you acting this way?"

Theo moves forward and is about to say something to his father.  Ben sees him and raises his hand and slaps him so hard that he almost falls.  Though only five years old, he doesn't cry, but holds his hand to the burning skin on his face.  "Why, Pawpaw?  I sang good.  I know I did."  He, finally, starts to tear up.  "I wuz good, Pawpaw."  He insists.

Carolyn goes to him.  "You were perfect Theo.  You also, Antonia.  Absolutely, perfect.  Don't let him tell you any different."  June gasps.  Carolyn has both the children under her physical protection now.

Will and Grant have both come forward to stand between Ben and his little ones.  Grant turns to the stunned group.  "I wasn't going to introduce them, but the two angelic voices that accompanied my wife, belong to Miss Antonia Johnson and Mr. Theo Johnson."  He looks at cousin Ben Ford.  "The proof is in the eyes."

Again, June gasps.  She comes forward.  "Children, who is your father?"  They both point to her husband.  "Who is your mother?"  They both answer at the same time, but name different mothers which makes June gasp and turn redder than Carolyn has ever reached.  She turns on a dime to face her husband.  "Ben, you owe me an explanation for all this."

Ben looks at her. "I don't owe you anything. Why would you believe these niggers? I told you that I didn't trust Grant. I have had enough! We are leaving." He roughly grabs June's arm.

June wrestles out of his grasp and puts her hand up to stop his rhetoric. She says in a loud stern voice that would make any child quiver. "Benjamin Theodore Johnson. These children are named after your parents. Theo said his mother was Molly. I remember Molly from your parents' household, as well as Sara. Sara was gone before Grant inherited. She left um . . . how old are you little girl?"

"Ten, ma-am."

"That's about right. She left about eleven years ago. Benjamin, say something." Ben did the opposite. He turned around and walked out the front door, without another word.

June takes a step toward the door. "Bennnnn!" She yells.

George, Ben's younger brother, steps forward. "June, what can he say? As Grant put it, 'the proof is in the eyes.' Let us take you to our home. This is a deplorable situation." He looks to Carolyn, but nods to the children. "Are they taken care of? Do they need for anything?"

Carolyn shakes her head. "They are now living in Lawrence. They each have a proper roof over their head and their mothers are now leading productive lives. We saw to it, immediately. We care about them, and their mothers, Uncle George. They are the true innocents, here."

Carolyn looks toward the kitchen and calls out. "Annabelle, come get Theo and put a cold compress on his face." When the large black woman takes both children with her, she repeats. "They are happy and will always be taken care of in Lawrence. You need never to see them again. They are being well attended to. The mothers seem very happy with their new situations"

"Good. Glad to hear it." He turns to Grant. "Was this the 'problem' that almost cost you a bride?" Grant nods. "Thank you for your trying to be discreet during dinner. Well, it was nice meeting you, Carolyn. You are a most gracious host, and you sing beautifully. Come everyone, I think this evening is over." He turns toward the door.

Carolyn goes to him. "Uncle George, we weren't going to tell anyone of their parentage."

Grant speaks up for the first time. "I knew that Ben wouldn't be able to just sit there. He immediately went on the defensive. But I swear, I wasn't going to say anything tonight."

"Well played, either way. Good night, all. Have a happy New Year." George takes his hat and coat from Clarence and walks out the door, without another word.

That was it, everyone started filing out. Lizzie, Ezra, Mary and Julia all go into the kitchen with plates and serving pieces to help clean up the dining room. The 'un-related' guests thanked the newlyweds for a very entertaining evening. Miles Curtis says, "I cannot wait to see what you have planned for the next get together! Oh, Boy, Howdy! And Happy New Year."

As she closes the door on the last guest, Carolyn sharply turns to her brother. "Why didn't you tell me the plan? Didn't you trust me? When did the children get here? What about their mothers? I cannot believe that they let you use them this way. This could have gone horribly wrong, you know. You had no right to use these children as pawns in your chess game. You are no better than Ben."

Julia walks back into the room. "Carolyn, that's not fair, as you said, we weren't going to tell anyone their identity. Will thought that Ben would show his hand having to be in the same room with them, the Reverend, his wife, brother and sister. The plan was, if he had kept quiet, Will or Grant would go to him later and threaten to go to Auntie June and say, 'Remember the children singing at Grant's party?' That's all. Ben saved Will that extra step."

"It just doesn't seem right. That poor little boy. Ben threatened to slap the boy, before. Grant, you should have been more protective of him. He is just a little boy! As a soon-to-be father, you should have had more sense. I am just so mad. I cannot talk to any of you anymore!"

She marches up the stairs to her room. Her first married dinner party was just a ruse to get even with the man that was blackmailing them. Ben is ruined and will not bother them anymore; which is nice, but why did it have to happen at *her* first dinner party? She can remember the horrified look on everyone's face. This will be the talk of EL Dorado for years.

147

What a way to start in a new Society. *How could they do this to me? I don't know who I am madder at: my brother Will or my husband. Of course, Julia was in on it also. I feel used. They didn't trust me enough to tell me the plan! If they, at least let me participate in the trap. I would feel like I lost my standing in Society on my terms, but I was a dupe as were my guests.* She is undressing in the Master suite when Grant comes into the room. He looks at her and she turns her back on him.

"Don't be mad at me, Carolyn. I would rather lose the Farm than your love. I didn't expect Ben to become unglued that way. I thought that he would keep his mouth shut and we would blackmail him, later." Her back is still to him and she is putting her jewelry away in her jewelry box. "Carolyn?" He needs her to look at him. "I blame you for the whole disaster." She spins around immediately.

"How?" She says. Her jaw is clenched and he knows that means she is about to explode.

"Your song. 'Away In The Manger' gave him a guilty conscience. Especially, with your Angelic voice. Then those children's voices added to it, was more than he could handle. Again, your fault. You taught them the song, perfectly. So, the whole kerfluffle is your doing. What do you have to say to that?" He stands defiantly, with his hands on his hips.

"My fault? You are saying this is my fault! Is that what you are saying?" Her jaw clenches back up, again.

"I am." He says as quietly as he can.

"Poppycock!" She says. "If you are going to place the blame. Blame the Christmas carol."

"Well, Carolyn's Christmas carol has saved the Farm, but ruined a dinner party! Which would you prefer?" He waits for her next diatribe. Instead, he sees her stance soften.

"That is it!" She smiles. "That is perfect! Oh, Grant you just named my new filly! She will be a huge winner. Carolyn's Christmas Carol will save the day!"

"So you forgive me then?"

"Oh - No! You will be experiencing my bad humor for quite a while. We are going to host another dinner party next weekend, and see how that goes. Then, we will have parties each weekend so that people will forget the first one. I will be someone 'well respected' in EL Dorado, if it bankrupts you!"

**148**

"If that is what it takes! I agree with my penance. Now say you are not mad at me anymore. I cannot take it if you stopped loving me."

"Silly man! My being mad at you has nothing to do with my loving you. I will <u>always</u> love you, but I can *not like* you at the same time. Geez, Grant, don't you know anything at all?"

"Apparently, not."

# TWENTY- NINE

## Monday, January 1ˢᵗ, 1883 in EL Dorado

Grant is watching his wife sleep on this first morning of the New Year. She was so mad last night. *What if she doesn't forgive me? I need do something to win her back. But what?"* She sighs and opens her eyes. He braces himself for her hatred.

She smiles. "Still watching me wake? I have told you to stop that. Come here and kiss me instead."

"There is nothing that I would like to do more." He moves over to her and takes her in his arms. "I have your permission, then?"

"Yes, Mr. Johnson. I cannot stay mad at you. Though, I was thinking . . ."

"Oh, that sounds expensive. Name it. What would you have me do or buy?"

"Well, I am too impatient to have dinner guests weekly. I do need to have something next week, but why don't we just host a ball, like Will does. Open it to the public, but sell tickets and have the proceeds benefit the hospital. We will be pillars of society! The community will have a great time and the hospital will get a new wing in our name or something. Everyone wins!"

"You've been thinking about this for a while."

"Well, without you holding me all night, I had time to think through the problem. You need to get on this right away. Oh, make it Valentine's Day Ball! That is only six weeks away. You have so much to do!"

"Well, I had better get started on it, then. Time to get up." He turns to get out of bed.

"Hold it, don't move Mr. Johnson, you are forgetting something."

"What is it?"

"Holding the Mrs., first!" She rolls over onto him and pins him down. "Never mind, I see I am going to have to take charge of this situation, myself."

"I do not know if we have time for this. So much to do! Everyone is leaving for home, today. Will and Julia are taking

150

the early train.   Lizzie and Ezra leave on the afternoon stagecoach. Then there is the new task that you've giving me.  I need to put together a whole ball in just six weeks.  I am only one man.  What is a man to do?"

"A man is going to make love to his wife and the soon-to-be the mother of his baby."

"Your wish, as always and forever, is my command.  I am at your disposal to do with as you wish, my Carolyn.  I mean - Mrs. Johnson."

## THE END

# ABOUT THE AUTHOR

Cherisse M Havlicek writes in the beautiful town of Bridgman, Michigan. She has been married for over thirty years to a now retired Chicago Police Officer. Raised in the suburbs of Chicago, she fell in love and married him in 1985. When he retired from the Police Force in 1999, they had a seven-year-old boy, Arthur, and a two-year-old girl, Alisse. They knew that they wanted to live in Michigan, where they had been coming up on weekends for many years.

Cherisse has had a very varied work experience. She was a Hairdresser, an interior landscape horticulturist, a clerk at Cook County Juvenile Court, and in Michigan she worked at the daily Newspaper. There, she went from a Route manager to Single Copy manager to the top producer in the Advertising Department while raising her children, and attending their sports activities. She also helped take care of her husband's elderly mother and his disabled cousin, who lived with them.

As they became 'empty nesters', her husband was diagnosed with Lewy Body Dementia with Parkinson's. She knew that she could no longer work full time outside of the home, but even part-time endeavors took her away from home, too much.

In September of 2016, her grown son, Arthur, found chapter one of a book she started in high school and gave her grief about not finishing it. She wrote the next forty-five chapters in eight months and her first novel *ANNA AT LAST* was complete. She didn't stop there, though. She wrote *THE LEWIS LEGACY* while her husband had his back surgery and during his rehab. The third installment in the A Present / Past Saga series - *JUSTICE FOR JOSHUA* was also written in 2018. This little novella was written while her husband spent a few weeks hospitalized in early 2019. She has also written a Children's Christmas story called *A SILENT NIGHT*. All these works are now available for purchase. She, obviously, is making up for lost time and has no plans to stop.

You can connect with her on her Facebook page:
Author – Cherisse M Havlicek

www.ingramcontent.com/pod-product-compliance
Lightning Source LLC
Chambersburg PA
CBHW030335020726
47493CB00004B/1285